FALLING FOR
MR LOVE

Downsizing Opens Many New Doors
To Love

Elsie and Bella Series
Book 1

DEE GIBSON

GIBSON PUBLISHING

Forward

Inspired by Mary and Valerie, in their retirement village lifestyle. 'Keep smiling girls.'

This book is written in Australian English.

Contents

Chapter 1

Old age always seems so far away, offering freedom to do whatever you like throughout the day. Unfortunately, it arrived unannounced one grey Melbourne morning as Elsie slid out of bed. It was meant to be a gentle movement to get her feet balanced. But the floor came up to meet her all too fast and it tossed her sideways. The harsh thud of her head hitting the carpet jarred her into unconsciousness. Elsie's body slumped to the carpet. As she lay there her daughter Emma's voice rang in her ears. *Mum get a portable alarm it's such a little price to pay for your safety.*

She had discussed it with her best friend Bella who thought they both should get one. They didn't go ahead and order an alarm as Emma suggested. They forgot about it.

Too late now, she thought as she laid on her back on the floor.

Pain tortured her legs. Her left foot was at a strange angle turned outwards and it would not move. Elsie opened her eyes, pain was raging through her body as her consciousness faded in and out. She could only stare at the ceiling her mind reacting to shock, a stark reminder of her vulnerability.

'Oh Hell' She said out loud. *How to get up?* She tried to move, one leg hurt more than the other. She tried to wiggle her bottom towards the door but nothing moved. Her mind gave her body instructions without response. She tried to pull at the edge of the bed clothes some of it slipped down to cover her middle. This expenditure of energy sapped her strength. Elsie's thoughts were fuzzy, she could not remember where she put her phone even though she could hear it ringing in the distance. Elsie tried again to pull herself along the floor, she made no progress. Hearing a thump outside her window at the front door, she thought she yelled, 'help! help! again convinced her voice was loud.

Surely who ever made the loud noise could hear her distressing calls. If she had her phone she could ring her best friend next door Bella and say, 'I can't get up.'

Pain pulsed at the top of Elsie's head, a dull throb beneath the sharper sting of something more sinister. Lifting a trembling hand, she touched her scalp, her fingers coming away slick and red. Blood. But where was the wound?

Her hair, usually soft and streaked with blonde high-lights, clung to her skin in matted strands. A grotesque mask of crimson smeared across her face, as if a child had taken a red Texta to it with careless strokes.

She lay motionless, her body sluggish and uncooperative. A memory surfaced, her younger self, feet pounding the pavement, wind rushing past as she outran the neighbourhood kids. Speed had once been second nature. Surely, some of that strength still remained?

She tried to move. A violent spasm shot through her

legs, stealing her breath. Panic tightened its grip. Logic wove its way through the haze, a cruel whisper at the edge of her mind. She was in trouble. Deep trouble.

She tried to concentrate. With the last of her energy she tried again to reach the bed clothes. They were too far away. The next time she woke she was shivering with cold.

In the distance Elsie heard her phone and recognised it was Emma ringing. *Bloody phone. I need to get to it.* These thoughts raced through her mind for the short time she was conscious.

Again, the mobile phone rang… Elsie tried to turn her head towards the hallway in vain. The third time it rang or so she thought, she heard the land line click through to the answering machine on. *Where are you Mum? I'm on my way to work just checking up on you.'*

Checking up' …. Elsie drifted off again, drained of any strength to even try to move her hands. She did not hear a key turning in the outer wire door, or the jangle of the key opening the front door. Bella her best friend yelled out, 'are you alright in there Elsie? Emma rang me to check on you.' Elsie recognised a familiar voice in a dream. She fought to open her eyes but everything had turned black.

As Bella discovered her friend in distress her scream of fright filled the house. She hurried to make Elsie as comfortable as possible, covering her with the bed clothes and carefully placing a pillow under her head.

Bella quickly dialled for the ambulance. 'You're going to get into a whole lot of hot water over this Elsie, no alarm and possibly a broken leg or hip. Emma will give you the rounds of the table for sure.'

Bella looked down at her best friend knowing full well she would not be able to help Elsie to get up. She had no trouble picking up the parcel that had been left on Elsie's front step as she came in, but Elsie wasn't a parcel.

Elsie was in and out of consciousness. Tiredness overwhelmed her as she floated in a dream state, her body immobilised. At times during this confusion, she was slightly aware of feeling like a burden, and could not grasp that her own body was betraying her. Elsie had lost any idea of where she was, as she slipped in and out of reality. She needed help, to point herself in the right direction. 'The phone,' she tried to say, it wouldn't come out.

Age awareness had also arrived at Bella's door a few months earlier, when she lost her house keys. Finding them in the fridge hours later became a secret she guarded even from Elsie.

Chapter 2

The ambulance arrived, sirens wailing as Elsie was rushed to the hospital. The world blurred into darkness, swallowing the journey, the hurried consultation with the Orthopaedic Surgeon, and the worried presence of her daughter, Emma.

When she finally opened her eyes, the room swam in soft, sterile light. A breathing tube rested uncomfortably in her nose, and a drip tugged at her arm. Instinctively, her hand drifted to her head, fingers meeting the rough texture of bandages.

Muffled voices murmured nearby—calm, reassuring— but she couldn't summon the strength to respond. Her body, heavy with pain medication, refused to obey. The emergency surgery on her hip had gone well, they must have told her that. Sleep had held her captive through the night.

A gentle pressure shifted the pillows behind her. The soft squeeze of a blood pressure cuff tightened around her arm. Then, with a swift rustle, the dividing curtain snapped open. Footsteps. Someone else was there.

'I feel… light… headed.' Elsie mumbled as she opened her eyes.

'It's shock,' a male voice answered her.'

'How long… have I...' Elsie tried to speak.

'You came in by ambulance yesterday morning. You have been sedated to avoid movement. I'm Doctor Collins, your Orthopaedic Surgeon. You had keyhole surgery to give you a new hip. Also a few stitches in the gash on your head. The worst is over.'

Elsie muttered. 'Better than … dead,' she answered faintly.

Dr Collins naturally thought the drugs were talking. 'The nurses tell me you've had visitors. By this afternoon you may even be awake enough to chat with them,'

He smiled with a caring bed side manner. 'The recovery is usually six weeks working with a physiotherapist, then onto careful walking. You'll be back on your feet sooner than you think. I'll be around to check on you tomorrow. Don't go anywhere.'

Elsie's eyes closed.

Emma and Bella were at her bedside at afternoon visiting hours.

Emma sat with a worried expression on her face. As an only child her responsibility level was high when anything went wrong with her mother. They were very close, as a schoolteacher, she was always organised. 'Mum, I'm so glad to see you awake,' Emma said. Bella softly patted her arm and held Elsie's hand.

'It's been no fun visiting you, a comatose patient with no sarcastic wisecracks.' Bella tried to keep the conversation light.

Elsie glanced around at her side table and weakly pointed at flowers and cards. 'Lovely,' she whispered.

Elsie's grandchildren, twins Sam and Stacey, had drawn her cards, which Emma had placed on the side table for her to admire.

'I will bring the kids in tomorrow afternoon to see you Mum, they send you hugs. We love you Mum.' said Emma, giving her a gentle hug.

The short visit over, Elsie closed her eyes in sleep.

Chapter 3

Elsie glared at that blasted wheelchair, her hands gripping its cold, metallic arms like it had wronged her personally. *Bloody thing,* she thought. 'Can't I try and walk?' she asked, though she already knew what the answer would be.

'Not likely,' the nurse replied, her voice chipper in that annoyingly patient way. 'I'm handing you over to rehab today. The nurses over there are bossier than me. They'll let you walk when they know you're ready.'

Bossier than you? Elsie bit her tongue. *I don't think so!* She scowled and muttered, 'Looking forward to that day.'

Rehab was twice a day, twice! but she was ready for it. Every time she lifted a leg or took a step, it felt like she was sticking it to the universe for putting her in this position in the first place. Each morning, she'd sit up, swing her legs out of bed, and just go for it. The thought of ditching that infernal wheelchair was all she needed to keep motivated.

And soon enough, she was up and down the small set of stairs in the exercise room. Elsie pushed herself and became more nimble than she'd expected for someone fresh from a hospital stint. When they finally sent her home loaded up with a walker, cane and painkillers, the real prize wasn't the physical recovery, it was freedom.

Emma, bless her, had filled the fridge with enough meals to last a decade. And every night, she'd show up after work to fuss over Elsie like a mother hen. For the first week, Elsie put up with it. But by the seventh evening, she'd had enough.

When Emma walked in that night, she found the table set, a steaming plate of dinner waiting, and Elsie standing proudly beside it, her walker parked off to the side.

'Time you had a break from coming here after teaching kids all day, Emma,' Elsie said as casually as she could, knowing full well her daughter would probably protest. 'I'm getting around just fine. I can manage.'

Emma tilted her head, still smiling but clearly confused. 'Really? '

'Of course, I'm fine.' Elsie waved her concern away with an exaggerated flourish. 'You've got a family to look after, and I've got Bella next door if I need anything. Besides, I wouldn't be game not to have my phone on me at all times.'

Emma didn't look entirely convinced, but she nodded anyway. 'Alright, but just ring me if you need anything, okay? I can always stop by on my way home.'

'Will do,' Elsie promised with a grin. 'And… I've even sorted out home delivery groceries today. No need to fuss.'

Emma laughed then, a warm, surprised sound that made Elsie feel just a little smug. 'You're back to your old self, using the internet and ordering home delivery.'

'Bella seems to think I need a different cake every day,' Elsie grumbled. 'Can you take some to the staff at school? My fridge is overflowing with cream sponge cakes.'

Emma's face lit up. 'Oh, they'll love that, and Stacey and Sam's favourite is the chocolate sponge cake Bella makes.'

'Of course, it is,' Elsie said with a chuckle.' That's the best one she does.'

Chapter 4

Elsie had a lot of time to think about her future now that she was home from the hospital. The days dragged by slowly, and today felt even worse. Perhaps it was delayed shock, or maybe it was just the loss of her independence, something she had fought tooth and nail to maintain. Either way, she'd woken up in a bad mood this morning, and it wasn't shifting. She glanced at the table, irritated at the few crumbs that had escaped from her mouth. Sweeping them into her hand, she let them fall into the saucer under her cup.

Bella had brought over a vanilla sponge cake, to cheer her up. *Bloody sponge cake*, Elsie thought, *as if that could fix everything.* Still, she knew she'd eat it, even with this bad mood hanging over her like a wet blanket.

'Did we ever think we would be here, Bella?

'Where?' replied Bella, taking a bite of sponge cake as if nothing was wrong. *Of course*, the bad mood made Elsie think the worst of everything. *Bella didn't have a care in the world.*

'Old age,' stated Elsie. 'Did we ever entertain a thought of us being old?'

Elsie stared out of the window for a moment. Old. The word itself felt foreign, like it belonged to someone else. She didn't feel old, not in her mind. Her body disagreed, of course, what with the walker and the constant aches. But inside, she was still the same Elsie as she'd always been, the one who used to race Bella to the shops and dance with abandon at every party. Where had *that, Elsie* gone?

Elsie sat at the kitchen table, her mind going over her life and her recent trip to hospital. Having to depend on others had rattled her. Shaking her head, Bella sipped her tea.' We were asleep at the wheel Elsie, and it just snuck up on us.'

Snuck up? Maybe for Bella. For Elsie, it felt like she'd been ambushed. One minute, she was living life on her own terms, and the next she was flat on her back in a hospital bed, with people telling her what to do. Well, she wasn't going down without a fight. Not yet. Not until she'd had her say. It was her life not Emma's.

'Well,' Elsie's voice was picking up steam, 'it's time to wake up. I'm bloody sure that Emma won't have control over my life. My money can stay safely in the bank. How would I know if she'd just up and buy a Porsche for her current husband, as soon as my eyes were closed for the last time.'

'He's a sweet talker, if ever I heard one. Anyway, Emma drives a Corolla,' Bella went on. 'I don't see her in a Porsche, Elsie. But then again, Todd might see himself in one. He's so egotistical.'

Elsie snorted, the image of Emma's stick-thin husband in a Porsche too absurd to ignore. But she couldn't shake the gnawing feeling of being pushed aside, of having her future decided for her. *What if they don't listen to me? What if they sell the house and dump me somewhere awful? I won't be able to fight back then. I won't…Elsie's brain was on a roll.*

Bella kept chatting, but Elsie barely heard her. She was too busy replaying every conversation she'd had with Emma, wondering if there was something she'd missed. Some sly mention of retirement homes or downsizing. She wanted control over her life, and if there was one thing Elsie hated, it was feeling like she didn't have control.

Elsie had conquered her physical recovery with steely determination. Realising that the time had come to downsize, blame had to be put on someone, and Emma copped it. Elsie's thoughts were out of proportion, she had entered a new beginning and it was raw and unacceptable. Fear and uncertainty had made her feel vulnerable. Elsie wanted to decide where she would live. If the end years were to be boringly away from her own home, she wanted to choose. This had been her home for forty years and she didn't want to leave it without an excellent alternative.

'It's going to be my end of term, not hers,' Elsie muttered. It sounded more bitter than she'd intended, but she didn't care. The words had been rattling around in her brain for days. They needed to be expressed.

Elsie kept making her point, 'You know how school-teachers love to have all their projects wrapped up by end of term. Well, it's going to be my end of term not hers.'

'Ok Elsie you've got the complaints department open today, get it all off your chest. Emma doesn't deserve this bad press Elsie, she is your daughter, and she loves you.'

'Oh yes, she does,' said Elsie.

'Well, grin and bear it. At least she remembers where you live.'

'Occasionally,' replied Elsie.

'My son William is in London and I'm lucky to get phone calls and photos of my granddaughter.'

'It's all I can think of, ' said Elsie, ignoring Bella.'

They usually laughed over morning tea. Finding life and its events a funny play. Today Elsie had more than a smidge of melancholy in her voice. Elsie sipped her tea, trying to distract herself.

Bella was right. Emma loved her. But loving wasn't the same as understanding.

Elsie frowned, 'Emma has already spoken with a Real Estate Agent, he is a friend of Todds. He will come to value the house when I am ready. Did I say I'm selling? Did I say I am ready to move? Well, I'm not ready.'

Elsie went on and on. 'Did you see that article in the paper about the food they serve in aged care homes? Five dollars a day. Couldn't feed a rabbit on that.'

Bella rolled her eyes. 'I think it's per meal, Elsie.' 'You are making this up as you go along. No one can make you do anything. I don't know anyone who would even try, for heaven's sake. You love a fight, and you are always right.'

'I am not!' said Elsie abruptly.

'Oh yes, you are, you silly old goose.'

Laughter broke Elsie's bad mood.

'You may have broken your hip, said Bella, 'but you still have all your marbles.'

'Well thanks. You keeping a tally, old girl? Suppose you have my mistakes written on your calendar.' Elsie's loud laugh filled the room.

They had been friends a lifetime, so nothing they said was off limits. 'I wasn't the one who looked up all the dementia tests online.' Bella declared.

'Well, how would I have known how to pass it? To think

we had to count backwards in sevens... God, doctors are sneaky.' Elsie rolled her eyes.

'Sneaky could apply to you, cheating and looking up all the answers before your appointment.' Bella shook her head.

'Well,' said Elsie, 'it helped you too, didn't it?'

Bella's face changed to surprise 'No, I could always count backwards.'

'Phooey! You could not. I've never heard you mention it. Elsie took a breath before continuing. 'Anyway, I should get extra points for being able to look it up on the computer.'

'No extra points, Elsie. You either pass or you don't.' Bella replied as she shrugged her shoulders.

'Well, I'm still driving. Not like someone I know' Elsie huffed.

'Oh, rub it in, go on, rub it in! It's my eyes, not my brain that stopped me driving,' Bella admitted.

'No.' said Elsie. 'I don't think so. Your son said it's time and your doctor agreed.'

Laughter bounced off the kitchen walls, mingling with the golden morning sunlight streaming through the window. Two women, armed with wit and steaming mugs of tea, sat across from each other, their conversation a delightful battlefield of sarcasm and quick comebacks.

No schedules. No obligations. Just the pure joy of verbal sparring, where the only rule was to outwit or be outwitted. One quip led to another, their imaginations twisting the mundane into the absurd until even the sugar bowl seemed to be in on the joke.

'You know, if we bottled our conversations, we could make millions.'

'Oh sure, right after the world finally appreciates the brilliance of tea-stained wisdom.'

Another burst of laughter. They weren't here to solve life's problems—just to mock them over a cuppa. Seriousness had no seat at this table, and frankly, it wouldn't have survived even if it tried.

Chapter 5

When Emma visited next, Elsie could feel it in the air, the topic of retirement villages circling their conversation like a vulture, waiting for the right moment to swoop. She had been bracing herself for this, anticipating the inevitable talk of new chapters and comfortable facilities. But Elsie wasn't one to sit back and let things happen to her.

Clearing her throat, Elsie decided to take the bull by the horns. 'I'll have you know Emma 'I'm choosing where I move to.' Her tone clipped but still playful. She studied her daughter's face, searching for the flicker of guilt or agreement. No point in dancing around it. Best to drag it into the open.

Emma's eyebrows lifted, as she smiled at her mother. 'Surprised, are you?' Elsie said watching her closely. She'd expected Emma to start nudging her towards some soulless place with beige walls and bad tea. But if Emma thought she was going without a fight, she had another thing coming.

'Well,' Emma said, laughter bubbling, 'that took some

bravery, bringing it up yourself. Mum, I have no intention of suggesting your next step in life, that's for you to find.'

They both chuckled, but Elsie's mind was already racing ahead. 'I'm going to get online and find the perfect place,' she announced. 'Bella's coming along for the ride, too.'

Emma tilted her head, amusement flickering behind her eyes. 'Bella?'

'Yes, she may even move in with me.' Elsie sat a little straighter, enjoying the reaction.

Emma held back a laugh, her lips twitching. 'And what exactly does Bella think of this?'

'Oh, she doesn't know yet,' Elsie admitted. 'She can't use a computer. I do worry for her, you know she might not have enough time left to learn spreadsheets.'

Emma snorted. 'Why on earth would Bella need spreadsheets?'

Elsie shrugged. 'She might.'

Emma shook her head. 'Mum, you don't even know how to use spreadsheets.'

Elsie lifted her chin. 'I could if I wanted to.'

Emma gave her that look, that amused, exasperated look that said she knew her mother was talking nonsense but wasn't going to argue about it.

'Doubt it,' she said.

Elsie smirked, but beneath the banter, a heavier thought pressed on her. Enough playing around. Time to get serious.

'Emma, I have worked out that I have enough money to buy a nice place' The words came out steadier than she felt. But the worry of decisions still gnawed at her. Emma didn't hesitate. 'Of course you do, Mum. Even Dad's superannuation is enough, and when you sell this house, you'll have double. So, it's not a question of money.'

Relief washed over Elsie, but it didn't settle the deeper fear. It was never about the money. It was about control. Leaving this house meant leaving a lifetime behind. It meant the end of an era, her era.

Emma stood, smoothing her skirt. 'Mum, we love you, and all we want is for you to be happy where you are. No one else can choose for you, you have to be content with where you go. It'd be great if Bella was in the same village. Let me know when you've found the perfect place.'

Elsie nodded, as Emma kissed her cheek and headed for the door. The conversation had gone differently than she expected. Emma wasn't trying to push her anywhere, her own imagination had run away with her.

But what's perfect, really? It wasn't just about facilities, views, or food. It was about finding a place where she could still be herself. Where she wouldn't disappear into someone else's idea of what an old woman should be.

As the door closed behind Emma, Elsie smiled to herself. Behind the smile was something solid, something unshakable the stubborn, unyielding determination of a woman who wasn't ready to be put in a box.

Any kind of box, no matter how nice.

Chapter 6

Elsie and Bella sat at the table, the computer screen glowing in front of them, displaying one retirement village after another. The images were all the same, white-haired couples with impossibly youthful bodies and dazzling smiles. Some were perched in golf carts, others clinking glasses of wine at sunset, and a few even floated serenely in an indoor pool.

Elsie narrowed her eyes. 'They all look a little too happy.'

'Too posed,' Bella agreed, though her gaze lingered on one of the pools. 'Still, that does look nice.'

Elsie smirked. 'Still got your black bikini, Bella?'

'Of course. And I've got more chance of wearing mine than you have yours. Your swimmers would probably fall apart in shock if you ever took them out of the drawer.' Bella smirked, eyes twinkling. 'You bought them at least ten years ago, and let's be honest, your figure's changed since then. They've probably shrunk out of protest.'

Laughter rippled through the room, effortless and familiar, the kind that needed no explanation.

Elsie scoffed, lifting her chin. 'Well, I'm sure I've worn them a couple of times.' She paused, then grinned. 'So, we'd better put a pool on the must-have list for our new lifestyle village.'

Bella leaned back, her fingers wrapped around her mug, the steam curling between them. She had always been striking—tall and effortlessly elegant, her black curls spilling past her shoulders, now threaded with soft strands of silver. Time had left its mark, but gently, as if knowing she'd wear it well. Her high cheekbones framed a face that had turned heads for years, but it was her warmth, the way she made people feel seen, that truly drew others in.

She had never been one to play on her looks, never needed to. Confidence rested in the way she carried herself, not in the reflection of a mirror. And that, more than anything, was what made her beautiful.

They scrolled through more options until, finally, one caught their attention. It had a thoughtful layout, decent amenities, most importantly, didn't look like it was trying too hard to sell a fantasy.

'This one has everything we need,' Bella said, tapping the screen.

'We'll check it out first,' Elsie decided.

With their list narrowed down to three, they spent the next week visiting each village, walking the grounds, and inspecting the so-called 'village lifestyle' on offer. Finally, they made their choice.

The units were pristine, lined up neatly side by side in the newly built village, their fresh paint catching the afternoon light. Bella and Elsie stepped inside for a second look, taking it all in. Bella ran her fingers over the smooth kitchen bench top, eyes gleaming as she pictured trays of cakes cooling in the sunlit space. The wide counters, the state-of-the-art oven—this was a baker's dream.

Floor-to-ceiling windows bathed the rooms in natural light, highlighting the plush new carpet beneath their feet. Elsie trailed behind, nodding in approval as she peeked into the ensuite. A walk-in shower, plenty of space—wide enough for a wheelchair, if it ever came to that.

But the real victory? No garden to wrestle with. The courtyard out back was compact, just enough room for a table and chairs on a patch of tidy fake grass. No weeds. No endless pruning. Just space to sit, sip tea, and enjoy the quiet.

And the location couldn't have been better—five minutes from Emma's house, close enough for spontaneous visits but with enough breathing room to still feel independent. The village itself offered every stage of care: independent living for now, community support when they needed it, and eventually, palliative care.

Elsie presented the findings to Emma, ever the pragmatist. 'Three levels of care,' she explained. 'Independent, assisted, and then the final boarding call.'

Emma sighed. 'Mum, do you have to be so morbid? You have years left.'

'Morbid? No, just practical. Better to have a plan than leave it to chance.' Besides, if she couldn't laugh about it, what was the point?

'Yes, I do have years left,' Elsie conceded, 'which is why I'm choosing. And Bella's happy with it because of the pool.'

Elsie glanced at the brochure in Emma's hands, her nose wrinkling at the title. *Retirement Ease Village.*

Emma caught the look and smirked. 'What's wrong with it?'

Elsie scoffed. 'Sounds like a banker named it. Boring. We're calling it Lavender Lane.'

Emma laughed. 'That's not even close to the name.'

'Doesn't matter. We've already renamed it.' Elsie folded her arms. 'We have decided on the two units side by side. And when the fateful day comes, we'll invest in an outdoor loudspeaker.'

Emma raised both eyebrows. 'A loudspeaker?'

'Of course,' Elsie said matter-of-factly. 'When one of us goes first, the other can make an announcement. *Attention, residents! Bella has taken the early flight to heaven.*'

Emma pressed a hand to her mouth, stifling a laugh.

Elsie shrugged. 'Might as well go out with a bang, or at least a public service announcement.'

'You're impossible,' Emma giggled.

'And a scammer,' Bella added. 'She worked over the real estate agent too.'

Emma perked up. 'Oh?'

Elsie grinned. 'He said he might not be confident in getting an extra two hundred thousand on our houses if they were sold together to a developer. So, I said we might not be confident in him being the right agent. That put the wind up him, and he got the extra price.'

Emma shook her head, amused. 'You really were born to negotiate.'

Elsie just smiled. Life was about negotiation, and she wasn't about to let it slip through her fingers now.

Chapter 7

Elsie and Bella started the big clean up and packing. 'There is more stuff here than I remembered,' Elsie frowned as she opened cupboards. 'We should have started earlier.

I hardly remember having all these books, and in the kitchen, I've got so many glasses I could host a wedding.'

Bella shook her head. 'Don't know if you are a hoarder or just plain lazy,'

'I haven't opened half of these cupboards for years, so it's probably laziness. You as bad, Bella?' Elsie said.

'Hate to admit it, but some of the things I have found could go in a museum. The local opportunity shop will make some cash out of them. But who uses doilies, and milk jug covers anymore?'

Elsie laughed loudly, 'Oh, I've won this contest. I have ancient invitations from weddings and old birthday cards from people I don't even remember. Why did I keep them? Who knows. I'm not sentimental, so I'm a lazy bones.'

Bella nodded in agreement.

'Not to mention my clothes. I started to look through

both wardrobes and some of the sizes are a joke, I'll never get into them again. Probably time to clear them all and buy a new range, I have the money to do it, but it keeps slipping my mind.'

'Don't think it slipped your mind. You just admitted you are too lazy.' Bella laughed and Elsie had to agree with her friend.

'You can't wait till things come back into fashion, Elsie, they won't fit anyway.'

'My bathers will still be ok. I've only worn them a couple of times.'

'The elastic will be perished by now. You need new ones.'

'No I don't, they are perfectly fine.'

'Fine for ten years ago,' remarked Bella.

Ignoring Bella's jibe about the bathers, Elsie decided on a break. 'Let's have a cuppa, Bella, it's more than I can face right now.'

'Good idea, but a better idea is to get someone to do it for us. They could do your house first, then mine.' Bella suggested half joking.

As they sat drinking more tea, they conceded that they needed help. Elsie looked through the computer listings for furniture removals.

'Listen to this one, Bella. 'We help you pack, and move your furniture to your new home, we also have a 'sweep clean service' to pack and discard your personal item, say yes or no, and it is completed in a few hours. That sounds great, doesn't it, Bella.'

'Exactly what we need.'Bella agreed.

'Sit in a chair and someone does the packing, sounds perfect' said Elsie, as she clapped her hands. Let's book them before they get away.'

'Final proof that we are both totally lazy.' Bella laughed.

Elsie made the booking and learned that the company also did the reverse at the new home; They unpacked and placed everything in cupboards neatly. Elsie didn't even ask the price.

'Bella, guess what… they are going to set up everything in our new units for us, isn't that great.'

Bella sipped her tea, closed her eyes and said 'Perfect.'

Chapter 8

Elsie and Bella lounged in the handkerchief-sized courtyard of Bella's unit. Bella's new outdoor furniture—sleek, modern, and perfectly arranged, was the last piece of the puzzle in her new home.

The moving trucks had long since rumbled away, leaving behind a space that was already tidy, every box unpacked and whisked away by the removalist's. The extra fee they'd paid for the full service had been worth every cent. No aching backs, no chaos—just a seamless transition into their fresh start.

Elsie stretched, letting out a satisfied sigh. 'Glad I thought of it.'

Bella shot her a look over the rim of her cup. 'Oh please, I was the one who said we needed help in the first place. You didn't just think it up out of nowhere.'

Elsie smirked, undeterred. 'Came up with the idea, did you, Bella? Well, I was the one who actually found the removalists.'

Bella rolled her eyes, but her smile gave her away. Some debates were timeless.

'I'm so happy we sold to the developer and got the extra price. It certainly made the agent work hard for his fee.' Elsie laughed.

'Well, I do admit that was one of your better ideas.' Bella smiled.

'Looking forward to happy hour tonight?' Elsie asked

'Yes, I wonder if everyone dresses up or goes casual?' Bella replied.

'Mmm I'm not sure, I haven't had a good look at the other inmates yet. It won't hurt to put on a bit of lippy and comb our hair.'

'Well, I look ok the way I am. I don't feel like changing clothes.' Bella smiled.

'Of course you don't,' laughed Elsie. Bella had never had to work hard to look impressive.

Elsie was shorter, curvy and plump, with light brown hair highlighted with blonde tips. She always had it cut in a modern style that was easy to manage. He face was very pretty, especially when she smiled or laughed. Her quick wit and loud personality took most people by surprise. Elsie was an acquired taste, and without a quick sense of humour you had little chance of being on the same page as her. She was often hilarious, with funny responses to every conversation. Smart and down to earth she made friends with the latest jokes, and a good dose of sarcasm. Elsie and Bella both loved fashion, and shopping. When asked for her fashion advice, Elsie always replied, 'You can't go wrong with a black pair of pants and a crisp white shirt, unless you are cooking bolognese sauce.'

THE CROWDED ROOM held more women than men, and a sign on the table just inside the door said, *champagne: first glass free.* Having a glass in their hands made them start to feel they belonged. Even though it had only been two days since moving in.

Watching as the crowd milled about in their finest clothes. Bella mentioned 'We should have put in more effort, just a bit of lippy wasn't going to cut it with this lot. They all look like they are at a wedding.'

'Well, hello ladies.' A short man with thinning hair, and average looks, sauntered over to them.

He looked them up and down, as if judging a cow or a bull at a country show. 'I'm Ted. Still unpacking, I, see?'

'Oh,' said Elsie with a slight frown, catching the sparkle in Bella's eye. *Poor man. He doesn't know what he's in for.*

'No, we had people unpack for us.' said Elsie. 'These are our meet ugly men clothes. We always wear them for a first meeting so we can sort the duds from those with manners.'

Ted's laugh was not loud, and his face had an odd expression mixed with a reddening of his cheeks. *Did she actually say that?*

They moved off and mingled themselves into a group of ladies discussing golf. After listening to endless golf stories, Elsie finally got a word in. 'This seems like a golf mad place.'

I'm Connie, 'Do you play?' She asked.

'We play, but not golf,' said Elsie giggled.

Bella elbowed Elsie in the ribs, and she rephrased her words smiling widely. 'No, I have never been able to play after my hip operation, and Bella swings too far to the right to find the flag.

One lady laughed and Elsie immediately liked her.

'Pity,' said Connie. 'We could recommend you to our golf club, we're always looking for new members.'

'Well what else is there to do here? asked Bella.

'Mahjong,' said one, 'craft,' said another.

'Nice' said Bella, 'but I'm not creative.

'Is there a community garden?' asked Elsie?

'No,' two of them answered together, both shaking their heads.

'Pity, we were hoping for at least a corner plot where we could grow our own special plants.' Price is going through the roof.'

The lady who laughed earlier this time bent over in a full belly laugh.

'I'm Pat,' she said. 'Come on, ladies. Let's introduce these two newbies around.'

'Thanks,' said Elsie. 'Newbies! Eh! That's what they called us in prison.'

'Heavens,' said one lady stepping back.

'It's alright. I only got three years. Caught bringing stuff back from Bali.' Elsie held a blank face.

'Bella looked ready to say something, but Elsie wasn't having it. She nudged her with an elbow, shutting her up before she could ruin the fun.' Elsie always got annoyed when Bella interfered with her when she was on a roll. 'Spoil sport.' Elsie whispered.

'They walked around doing the meet and greet, a smile here and there and a good checking out of clothes. Elsie and Bella checked out all the men's clothes, to see who had been dressed by their wife, ironed perfectly with creases straight.

'It's nice to get the champagne for free on the first night,' said Elsie to one of the custodians of the champagne bottle, as she got her glass topped up. Her astonished expression was involuntarily. 'Oh no it's the first glass free, then it is five dollars a glass after that. You put the money into the honesty bowl. The word honesty bowl stuck in the poor woman's throat. 'You have to pay for it,' she rephrased the words. It was the way she said honesty bowl that gave Elsie a way in, 'It's ok I wasn't in for theft, love, I'll bring the money next time.'

They stayed for one hour, it was all they could take of such a self-absorbed group of new friends. Elsie said to one named Nola, 'You will have to excuse us. Ted noticed and commented on our dress code, thinking we were in our gardening clothes. We are feeling a little conspicuous, so, we'll call it an early night.'

'Don't take any notice of him.' Replied Nola.

'Is this on most Friday nights? asked Bella.

'Yes, every week, always at five.' said Nola.

Bella smiled and replied, 'Good. We'll be here next week dressed to kill.'

Bella and Elsie belly laughed all the way back to their units. 'What an odd lot of inmates,' said Elsie. 'Reckon they have been locked up for too long?

Bella smiled at Elsie's remark. 'Definitely made you happy to find a whole new group to terrorise, Elsie. I'm so embarrassed. '

'Oh, what rubbish, Bella. When have you ever been embarrassed?' 'When you said you had been in jail, what-ever must they think?' They both giggled.

'There's a lot of humour training to be done and tonight it started. They have a long way to go. Good to make an interesting first impression.'

'By the way, Bella when are we getting back to golf?'

Never! I swing far too much to the right, or am I the

one with the bad hip? 'No that's me.' Elsie chuckled, 'We'd better get our stories straight.'

'Bloody hell that would be too normal,' said Elsie.

They finished the night with a bowl of pistachios and a large glass of Baileys to toast their first inmate get together.

Chapter 9

Elsie had not yet settled into her new bed. All the different noises and creaking in the building un-nerved her. She'd just closed her eyes waiting for sleep when she heard a noise. A male voice right outside her unit? Surely not.

Then a little tap, tap, on her window.

'Are you awake?' The male voice asked. *A male voice at my window I don't believe it.* Elsie pulled the covers back and stealthily got out of bed. She had no idea who it could be. She tiptoed to the window, peeking out through the corner of the blind. She saw Ted from happy hour.

What the bloody hell does he want?

'Are you awake?'

Tap! Tap! On the window. 'Annie, Annie, I'm outside,' he said.

Well, this wasn't Annie's house, and he was obviously trying to connect for a fling. Elsie remembered when they signed up for the unit, being told that there was a safety button in each unit that went straight through to the night guard in case of emergency. It was on the wall in the kitchen. She crept out in the darkness through the lounge room and around to the kitchen wall. Running her palm flat along the wall, she found the button. She pressed it without a thought. A siren sounded throughout the village; it was ear-piercing. Lights came on one after the other in the units.

The resulting siren shattered the night's silence, blaring loud enough to wake the entire village. Lights flicked on across the neighbouring units, one after another. Elsie winced at the noise. *Bloody hell, that's loud enough to wake the dead.*

She flicked on her own light and stormed out her front door. In her nighty and bare feet. Ted was still there, looking thoroughly confused.

'What are you doing at my window?' Elsie yelled, her voice carrying across the gathering crowd of neighbours.

Ted stammered, but before he could get a word out, Elsie pressed on. 'What the hell do you think you're doing? Annie isn't here—this is my unit!'

Nearby, Bella doubled over in laughter, her cackles echoing into the night. Elsie's indignation only grew. 'Don't you dare try to tell me you came over to borrow a cup of sugar,' she bellowed, glaring at Ted.

Ted began backing away, looking for all the world like a guilty schoolboy caught red-handed. 'Where am I?' he mumbled, playing dumb.

'The poor bloke didn't know what trouble he had met.

'Now don't try and tell me you came over to borrow a cup of sugar.' Elsie bellowed.

Ted tried to move off backwards, playing his idiot card. 'Where am I?'

His wife Dulcie came hurrying around the corner. 'Does he belong to you?' Elsie roared.

'Ted, why are you out here.'

'Knocking on my window looking for Annie.' Elsie barked. She had an audience and made the most of the drama. Elsie wasn't about to leave any details out.

A lady in the unit next to Bella went inside and turned off all her lights. Elsie guessed that was Annie's unit.

'Ted, get back home.' Dulcie sounded off. She looked at the gathered crowd and said loudly, 'Dementia.'

Elsie snorted.' More like fornication.'

A golf cart rounded the corner at full speed, the Village Manager, Michael, at the wheel. Elsie folded her arms as he screeched to a stop.

Elsie stared in disbelief, 'taking golf a bit far this time of night isn't it Mick?' she said.

'It's Michael not Mick, what's the trouble Elsie?'

'Ted was knocking on my window calling out to Annie. Dulcie is walking him home now.'

'I'll check on them on the way back'

'Thanks, Mick.' Elsie said.'

'We should have gone to the information night on the rules of the village; we might have been told that the button is attached to a siren,' said Bella

'You know I don't do boring information nights, I'm more of a learn on the job kind of girl.' Elsie giggled.

'Loud learning on the job,' Bella laughed.

Bella wandered into Elsie's unit, both of them wrapped in dressing gowns, their hair slightly disheveled from the interruptions of the night. They settled at the kitchen table, steaming cups of tea in hand, a plate of chocolate-coated Tim Tams between them. Conversation flowed easily, weaving between memories, mischief, and the lingering chaos of the night.

Laughter spilled into the quiet kitchen, soft and unrestrained, pushing away any tension that remained. Outside, the first hints of dawn crept through the window, but neither of them cared. Some nights were meant to be stretched to the very last moment.

Chapter 10

Emma and the twins arrived carrying two large bunches of flowers to welcome Elsie and Bella to their new homes. Emma barely stepped through the door before announcing, 'Didn't take me long to drive here. Maybe five minutes.'

Elsie nodded. 'Yes, that makes it easier for you.'

'Todd not able to visit us today?

'No he is doing overtime again, you know how busy running a department can be.'

Meanwhile, Emma's twins Sam and Stacey were already on the move, flinging open every cupboard and drawer in both units, inspecting their grandmother's new home like tiny property moguls. Finally, they deemed it acceptable. Sam and Stacey were twelve now and getting a good idea of life. Emma and Elsie allowed them to listen to adult conversations, so when Elsie started telling the story they were very attentive to every detail.

'Your unit is cool Nana,' Stacey declared.

'Have you met any of the residents yet?' Emma asked, settling into a chair. Emma was well dressed in modern jeans, boots and a navy and white striped polo top. She looked a lot like Elsie, except for her dark brown hair.

Elsie sighed, already preparing for the retelling. 'Oh, it was a bit of a shock at our first Friday night drinks,' she began, pausing just long enough to build suspense. 'I suggested we dress up, but Bella said no, just some lippy and a quick comb through our hair.'

Bella shot her a familiar look, tilting her head, with her hands on her hips she spoke in a defensive tone. 'Don't blame me Elsie, it was the other way around.' Your exact words were, 'Don't worry about dressing up, and look at the trouble that caused.'

Elsie rolled her eyes, but before she could protest, Bella turned to Emma. 'Your mother has already started wild rumours.'

Emma, entirely unsurprised, smirked. 'I'm not shocked. She can't help herself.'

Elsie leaned forward, her tea cup resting in her hands, eyes twinkling as she recounted the night's chaos.

'I was just drifting off to sleep, when I heard it, tap, tap on my window.' She mimicked the sound with her fingers against the table. 'Then a man's voice, low and urgent, calling, 'Annie? Annie, are you there?''

Emma's eyes widened. Bella smirked knowingly.

'I peeked through the blinds,' Elsie continued, her voice dropping for dramatic effect. 'And there he was. Ted. The grumpy one from Friday night drinks, the bloke who had the nerve to comment on our casual dress code.'

Emma snorted. 'No.'

'Oh, yes.' Elsie nodded, relishing the moment. 'And I knew exactly what he was up to, so I grabbed my dressing gown and headed to the kitchen in the dark.'

Bella spoke as she picked up her tea from the coffee table. 'She didn't hesitate. Straight to the security button.'

Elsie waved a hand. 'Well, I vaguely remembered something about a button in the kitchen. You know, for emergencies. And I figured a rogue pensioner looking for a late-night fling outside my window qualified.'

Sam and Stacey collapsed into laughter, sprawled on their stomachs, propped up on their elbows, eyes gleaming with anticipation.

Elsie leaned in, lowering her voice like a master storyteller. 'So, I crept through the dark,' she said, acting it out with exaggerated gestures. 'Ran my hand along the wall, found the button, and pressed it.'

She paused for dramatic effect, her expression turning innocent. 'Now, did anyone bother to tell us that button was connected to a siren loud enough to wake the entire lifestyle village?'

The room erupted with laughter, the kind that made stomachs ache and eyes water.

Bella smirked. 'They might have. But someone…' she shot Elsie a look, 'said information nights were boring.'

Emma shook her head, already laughing.

'Anyway,' Elsie continued, 'one by one, lights started flicking on. The whole place lit up like Christmas. And there I was, clutching my dressing gown to my chest, wondering if I'd just given myself a heart attack instead of scaring off Ted.'

Emma wiped away a tear. 'A booty call? At his age? I don't believe it.'

'Neither did I,' Bella said. 'Didn't look like he had it in him.'

'Oh, he had something in him,' Elsie said. 'A misplaced sense of confidence.'

The twins were now sprawled out on the floor, clutching their stomachs with laughter.

Emma leaned in. 'So what did you do?'

Elsie's grin widened. 'I flung the door open in my nightie and dressing gown and bare feet and gave him a proper earful.'

Bella nodded. 'The poor bloke didn't know what hit him.'

Elsie dropped her voice into a growl. 'Don't try and tell me you came over to borrow a cup of sugar!'

Emma howled.

Ted, according to Elsie, had stumbled back, blinking like a man waking from a particularly bad dream. 'Where… where am I?'

'And just when I thought it couldn't get any better, around the corner comes his wife, bathrobe flapping.' Elsie leaned forward. 'Ted?' she says, all shaky. 'What are you doing out here?'

Bella took over. 'And of course, Elsie, never one to downplay a bit of drama, points at him and declares, 'He was knocking on my window, calling for Annie.'

Emma gasped, delighted.

'And Dulcie, oh, the poor woman her face twisted in horror.' Elsie took a dramatic sip of tea. 'She looks at me, looks at him, looks at the entire audience of nosy neighbours now gathered around, and stutters, 'Dementia.''

Elsie sniffed. 'More like fornication.'

By now, Emma was doubled over.

'Oh, but it gets better,' Elsie said. 'Just as Dulcie's dragging him off, a golf cart screeches around the corner like something out of a cop show.'

Sam and Stacey perked up. 'No way.'said Sam.

'Oh yes. And who's driving? The Village Manager,

Michael. Looking way too serious for a man in a glorified golf cart.'

Bella smirked. 'And what did you say, Elsie?'

Elsie shrugged innocently. 'Taking golf, a bit far at this hour, aren't you, Mick?'

Emma covered her face.

Bella grinned. 'He didn't like that.'

Elsie shook her head. 'His jaw tightened. 'It's Michael, not Mick. What's the trouble?'

She gestured vaguely toward an imaginary Dulcie. 'Ted was looking for Annie.'

Bella finished the story with a smirk. 'Michael sighed, nodded, and said, 'I'll check on them on the way back.'

Elsie sat back, smug. 'And that's how I became acquainted with the official village alarm system.'

Emma wiped her eyes. 'Mum, you *cannot* make fun of old people.'

Elsie gasped. 'Make fun? Emma, some of the inmates in this place have forgotten what fun even is. I'm just reminding them.'

'I'm never getting old,' Stacey announced.

Sam grinned. 'Can I meet them?'

Elsie smirked. 'Oh no, you'd laugh way too much.'

Chapter 11

Ted had always noticed Annie, the widow living a few units down. There was something about her quiet nature, a shyness that drew him in. He started looking for reasons to run into her, little excuses to close the gap between her solitude and his restlessness.

The day the delivery truck left bare-rooted roses on Annie's doorstep, Ted was ready. He wandered over, hands in his pockets, as she stood studying the plants with a furrowed brow.

'Need a hand planting those?' he asked casually, though his pulse quickened when she looked up and smiled.

'That would be lovely,' she said, her voice soft and warm.

Before long, Ted was kneeling in the soil, digging holes while Annie chatted. She laughed at his stories, the sound bright against the quiet hum of the retirement village.

'This is so nice of you, Ted,' she said as he patted the last rose into place.' I don't know how I'd have managed without you.'

Ted grinned, wiping dirt from his hands. 'I love gardening,' he said. It wasn't exactly a lie, though it wasn't entirely the truth, either.

A few days later, Annie appeared at his door with a chocolate cake wrapped neatly in foil. Dulcie, his wife, opened the door, her expression tightening when she saw the cake.

'There's no need for that,' she said, walking off.

Ted stepped in quickly, taking the cake with an easy smile. 'Thanks, Annie,' he said, peeling back the foil. 'He broke a piece off, and took a bite. Best chocolate cake I've ever tasted.'

'Is that so?' Dulcie called from the kitchen. 'Funny, that's what you said about my chocolate cake. Back when I used to cook.'

Ted shot her a look, heat rising to his face. 'Used to, being the key phrase,' he snapped, his voice sharp enough to cut.

The cake was gone within a day, but Ted didn't need excuses like that anymore. When Annie mentioned in passing that one of her roses wasn't thriving, Ted was quick to offer his help. He brought over fertiliser and spent an afternoon in her garden, the air filled with the scent of soil and flowers.

'You should come see my roses sometime,' he said as he packed up his tools. 'I'll show you the proper way to prune them.'

Annie agreed, and the next day she stood in his garden, her fingers brushing delicately over the blooms. They talked about rose care, their conversation easy and unhurried. Ted barely noticed Dulcie watching from the window until the door banged open.

'You've never been a gardener,' Dulcie snapped,

marching into the yard. Since when do you know anything about roses?

Annie mumbled an excuse and slipped away, leaving Ted alone to face the storm. Dulcie's accusations flew like daggers, each one sharper than the last. Their marriage had been brittle for years, and now it was shattering under the weight of everything unsaid. For the first time, Ted didn't fight to pick up the pieces.

Later, he found himself standing in Annie's doorway, his chest tight with nerves. 'Do you think,' he asked, his voice hesitant, 'I could stay here? With you?'

Her answer came without hesitation. 'Yes, 'she said, her eyes kind.' Of course.'

Bit by bit, Ted moved in. A pair of shoes here, a set of tools there.

For the next few weeks, more and more of Ted's belongings found their way to Annie's unit. Clothes, shoes, tools and odd magazines mysteriously appeared at her doorstep in the middle of the night. Ted returned to Dulcie unit one last time, trying his key in the lock, only to find it didn't work anymore.

'The locks have been changed,' Dulcie called from behind the closed door. Ted knocked and Dulcie opened the door, passing him a box which he took and nearly dropped.'

'Have you been drinking Ted? She asked.

'Slightly, a bit.' He answered.

'Divorce? She asked her voice steady.

'Yes.' he replied, unsure of what else to say as he lent up against the door jam. Then he noticed something he had never seen before. Dulcie was crying.

'Sorry.' Ted muttered, not sure how to feel.

'Don't be,' she said wiping her tears.' These are tears of relief.'

———

ELSIE AND BELLA were out for a stroll, their conversation punctuated with chuckles. 'Is that Ted?' Elsie said out loud nudging Bella's arm.Her gaze was fixed on a figure weaving unsteadily down the path toward them. Elsie squinted. Sure enough it was Ted.

His ruddy face was flushed and his gait was uneven, outwardly he looked like he had had one drink too many. He was lugging a cardboard box that had seen better days, with the contents threatening to spill out with every step.'What on earth is he doing now?' Elsie muttered, more to herself than to Bella.

As they approached, Ted spotted them and halted in the middle of the path, trying to maintain his balance. 'Ladies.' He called out slurring slightly. A sheepish grin crossed his face.

'Ted,' Elsie greeted curtly, eying the box, revealing a mess of clothing, books, and what looked like an ancient alarm clock poking out of the top.' Annie's place,' he said nodding towards her unit.

'Annie?' Elsie's eyebrows lifted and a frown join in. Elsie and Bella exchanged a glance. Annie, the quiet widow who lived next door to Bella. To hear Ted was moving in with her was as surprising as it was intriguing.

'Yep,' Ted continued, clearly oblivious to the shock on their faces. 'She's got the best rose garden in the whole village, you know…'

'And well, Dulcie has made it quite clear I'm not welcome anymore.' At the mention of Dulcie, Elsie pursed her lips. Rumours about Ted and Annie had been circulating for weeks but seeing him here half drunk and hauling a box of belongings, confirmed what everyone had suspected. 'Does Dulcie know about this?' Elsie said crossing her arms.

'Oh she knows,' Ted relayed with a bitter laugh. 'Changed the locks on me last week. Gave me this box as a parting gift.' He paused, shifting uncomfortably under Elsie's sharp gaze.

'Anyway, Annie is happy to have me.' Ted said proudly.

Ted adjusted the box, a shirt sleeve now poked over the edge. 'Well I had better be going, don't want to keep the lady waiting.' He said offering them a half-hearted salute, before continuing his uneasy march toward Annies unit.

Gossip moved faster than Ted could, and soon everyone knew his story. Annie stayed by his side, tending to her roses as if nothing had changed. Dulcie kept her distance, her unit dark and uninviting.

Elsie and Bella stood in silence for a moment, watching as Ted continued walking.

'Well!' Bella finally said, breaking the silence. 'That explains the late night deliveries.'

'And the chocolate cake story must be true.' Elsie said dryly.

'Do you think Dulcie will stay quiet about this?

Elsie shook her head. 'Not a chance. This is going to be the talk of the village by dinner time.'

With that the two women resumed their walk, their conversation now focused on dissecting every detail of what they'd just witnessed.

As far as Elsie was concerned, the drama was just beginning.

A week later Ted received a letter in the mail from

Dulcie solicitor confirming the divorce proceedings had been started. Then the next day police knocked on Annie's door delivering an intervention order. Stating Ted must stay away from Dulcie and her unit.

'This is going to be tricky,' Ted said, rubbing his forehead. 'We're only eight units apart.'

'Do your best,' the officer replied, as he stepped off the porch.

Chapter 12

By the time Elsie and Bella arrived at Friday night drinks, the tension in the air was thick enough to slice with a butter knife.

Bella spotted the division immediately—two tables, two camps. On one side, Ted and Annie, flanked by their newfound allies. On the other, Dulcie, left to pick up the pieces. It was a mess. And Bella hated mess.

Elsie, on the other hand, practically thrived in it.

Bella gave her a sidelong glance, already predicting what was about to happen. Elsie was smiling too broadly, too cheerfully as if she were strolling into a Sunday picnic rather than a social battlefield.

'Well, isn't this a nice kettle of fish,' Elsie announced as they sat down, her voice light, her expression all innocence.

Bella winced. 'Oh no.'

Annie's shoulders hunched, her gaze fixed firmly on the table. Poor thing. She wasn't built for this kind of scrutiny. Ted, however, straightened, his expression hardening.

Then Elsie struck.

'I still can't believe you were knocking on my window,' she said, shaking her head in mock disbelief.

Bella stifled a laugh, because honestly, the image of Ted lurking outside Elsie's window was objectively funny, but a glance around the table told her they were the only ones who thought so.

'This is not a laughing matter Elsie,' one of the men muttered, his tone clipped.

'Bloody hell, it certainly is,' Elsie shot back. 'You think people aren't laughing behind their curtains at this latest tryst?'

Bella felt her stomach tighten at the word tryst. Too sharp. Too pointed. And Annie, poor Annie, was curling further into herself, her cheeks burning.

Ted sat up straighter, bristling. 'It's not a tryst. We're living together.'

The words dropped like a stone between them. Bella caught the quick flicker of something on Annie's face. Doubt? Regret?

Elsie, undeterred, grinned. 'Hold tight, Annie. I might have a rope in my garage you can tie him to your house, keep him from wandering again.'

Bella realised Elsie had gone too far. 'Okay, that's enough.'

'Elsie,' she said, in a firm voice. 'Ease off. You're way over the top tonight.'

Elsie let out an exaggerated sigh, picking up her wine glass. 'Fine, fine,' she said, waving a dismissive hand. 'I'll go. Don't want a police warning turning up at my door.'

Bella was already on her feet. She wasn't sticking around to watch this train wreck unfold any further. As they walked to the other table, Jan raised an eyebrow. 'You two get kicked off the island?'

Elsie huffed. 'I made a joke. It went down like a lead balloon.'

Bella barely suppressed a groan. 'Of course it did, not everything is a joke Elsie.'

Dulcie sat quietly at the next table, her eyes downcast. She looked... smaller, fragile. Nothing like the sharp, confident woman Bella had known just a week ago. Elsie slid into a chair beside her, tone uncharacteristically soft. 'How are you feeling, Dulcie?'

Dulcie let out a slow breath. 'We were married twenty years,' she murmured, barely audible over the chatter around them.

A sympathetic sigh rippled through the group.

'Oh dear, you poor thing,' one of the golf ladies cooed, her voice full of practiced pity.

Elsie scoffed. 'Don't give her sympathy,' she declared. 'She's probably relieved to be rid of him. I know I would be.'

Bella cringed. The conversation screeched to a halt. Faces around them tensed.

Elsie, apparently oblivious to the discomfort she'd just caused, took a sip of her drink.

Bella pressed a hand to her forehead, feigning a headache. 'Elsie, I think we should go.'

Elsie blinked at her, caught off guard.

Bella held her gaze. Let's go. Now.

To her credit, Elsie took the hint. 'What time is Mahjong?' she asked as they stood up.

'Monday at one,' someone replied, tin a clipped tone.

Elsie raised an eyebrow. 'All women?'

'Of course,' Pam answered with a prim smile.

'Well, count us out,' Elsie declared, flashing a mischievous grin. 'We're on the lookout for a man each.'

Bella's eyes widened. Oh no. No, no, no.

Elsie wasn't done.

'Preferably someone with money and a car,' she added, voice ringing out loud enough to carry across the room. 'So we can go out for lunches and dinners.'

A collective gasp rippled through the tables. Some looked scandalised. Others downright horrified.

Bella grabbed Elsie's arm, steering her toward the exit.

'You definitely made things worse tonight,' she hissed.

Elsie chuckled, completely unbothered.

'They think we're after their husbands,' Bella whispered.

Elsie only smirked. 'Well,' she said breezily, 'let them worry about it.'

Chapter 13

Elsie and Bella caught a taxi to the local Sunday market, held in a park a few kilometres from the village. As they wandered through the stalls, Elsie marvelled at the strange array of things she had no interest in buying. Crocheted baby clothes, aprons with Barb-B-Cue in bold letters, and handmade tea towels with little loops for hanging on the outside of the oven. Each stall seemed to offer something more bizarre than the last.

These are nice, Elsie said, eyeing a particularly hideous crocheted tea towel while casting a knowing look at Bella. The poor stall owner beamed proudly, oblivious to Elsie's true thoughts: *These clash worse than my aunt's old curtains.*

The rich aroma of coffee caught her attention, and they joined a line for cappuccinos. Once they had their cups in hand, they found a seat and took a moment to rest.

'There are more dogs here than people,' Elsie commented, watching as fur babies of all shapes and sizes paraded by with their proud owners.

They ran into another group from the village, standing

chatting. Alf had a jar of honey in his hand. 'Best honey ever over there,' He pointed, toward a stall covered in bee-themed decor. 'The Beekeeper sells it straight from the hive.'

'Nice fresh honey.' Said Elsie.

Elsie shrugged and made her way over to the stall, selecting a jar of golden honey. 'Might as well grab some,' she said, handing the Beekeeper the cash. As they walked, she couldn't resist unscrewing the lid and dipping her finger into the honey for a taste.

A familiar accented voice spoke next to them. 'Need a ride?' It was Hank, a widower from the village.

'Why not?' Elsie grinned, but her amusement dimmed slightly as she noticed Hank gravitating toward Bella, as they all walked towards his car.

Elsie and Bella both climbed into the back seat. Hank gave a disappointed look as he shut the car door of his new Mercedes.

'Not much of a market, really. She lifted a jar. 'I bought some honey.'

'I didn't spend a cent,' Bella chimed in.

Elsie shot her a teasing look. 'That's your training from being captive,' she said lightly, catching Bella's eye with a smirk.

Bella gasped dramatically, lowering her head and putting on a mock look of sorrow.

Hank glanced at Bella in the rear vision mirror, his brow furrowing. 'Bella, are you upset?'

Elsie didn't miss a beat. 'Of course she is,' she said, her tone shifting to something overly serious. 'She never gets over it when I mention the past. The psychiatrist said I should keep reminding her, you know, to help her process it.'

Hank glanced over his shoulder, concerned. 'Bella, are you upset?'

Hank frowned, taken aback. 'How unusual,' he said slowly. 'But you're cruel, Elsie. Bella deserves a chance at repatriation.'

Bella covered her face with her hands, barely containing her giggles.

'Exactly,' Elsie said, trying to keep a straight face.

When Hank pulled up outside Bella's unit, he got out and hurried around to open her door. 'There you go, Bella,' he said, smiling as he helped her out.

'Thank you, Hank,' Bella replied sweetly.

Elsie, already sliding across the backseat, waved him off.' No need for all that. I'll just slide across.'

'No, please, Elsie. I'll come around to your door,' Hank insisted.

'Don't bother, I'm almost there,' Elsie said, as she slid across the seat. Just as one foot was out of the car, disaster struck. The jar of honey slipped from her hand, and the lid popped off, sending a sticky stream of honey down her skirt.

'Bloody hell, now that Beekeeper's going to have to work overtime to collect more honey from his hives so I can replace it!' Elsie squawked.

'I've got it,' Hank said, reaching for the jar, but stopped when he saw the honey-soaked mess. 'Oh hell.'

Elsie glanced down at her dripping skirt, horrified. 'I thought I tightened the lid after I had a taste!'

Bella, meanwhile, had her back turned, her whole body shaking with silent laughter.

'Bella, get me a cloth, will you?' Hank asked, glaring at Elsie. Honey had smeared onto the door, her leg, and was now pooling on the carpet.

'I'll get the jar,' Elsie offered.

'No, leave it,' Hank snapped, his voice tight with frustration.

They both lunged for it at the same time, their hands fumbling, sending the jar tumbling to the tarmac, where it shattered. Hank's face twisted in disbelief, like a cricketer missing an easy catch.

Elsie bit her lip, holding back a laugh. Honey dripped from her skirt onto the road, Hank was visibly shaking, and Bella's stifled laughter wasn't helping.

'I'm sorry,' Bella whispered, returning with a towel. 'It's not your fault, Bella,' Hank replied, as he took the towel.

Elsie, never one to admit defeat, yelled, 'Honey washes out with plain water. I'll grab the hose!'

'No!' Hank barked, his patience snapping. 'Leave it alone!'

Ignoring him, Elsie headed straight for the hose in Bella's front garden, determined to clean the mess. But halfway there, she tripped over on the lawn, letting out a startled scream as she planted face-first into the grass.

Hank, without a word, continued picking up the glass with the towel, dumping it in Bella's rubbish bin. He shut the car door and drove off, without even glancing back.

Bella wandered over to Elsie, now still lying on her back on the grass. Bella gave her a gentle kick. 'You've really done it this time. We'll both end up in remand.'

Elsie roared with laughter. Together, they shrieked and cackled, Elsie finally pulling herself up with the help of the hose tap. Bella dashed into her unit, probably to avoid wetting herself from laughing too hard.

Later, they ordered Uber Eats, sitting in Elsie's unit, cracking jokes about toast and honey, and laughing until their stomachs hurt.

Hey Bella, 'what do you call a bee that's a poor looser?

'A cry bay – bee.' Laughed Elsie.

'I've got one,' giggled Bella. 'What's black and yellow and flies at 30,000 feet.'

'Go on,' grinned Elsie.

'A bee on a plane.'

Wait, wait, Bella threw her head back and stifled a laugh. 'Why did the bee get married'

'Oh Why'

'Because he found his honey.'

Eventually they ran out of jokes.

Chapter 14

Bella had been saying for weeks that they ought to have some fun, and today, she finally had an idea.

'You know, the one place we might actually enjoy ourselves is the pool,' she said, glancing at Elsie.

Bella smirked. 'Elsie, do you know where your bathers are?

'Of course I do!

Bella smiled, 'Didn't you throw those old ones out when you were packing?'

'They are in the bedroom drawer, and they still fit,' Elsie replied with more confidence than she felt. Truthfully, she hadn't tried them on in years.

Elsie gave her a knowing look. 'And does your black bikini still fit?'

'Of course! I've kept my figure,' Bella said with that air of smugness she did so well.

Elsie rolled her eyes. 'Well, yes, you've always eaten like a bird.'

'No, Elsie. I'm just naturally fine-boned.'

'Sure, like Royal Doulton bone china,' Elsie muttered, chuckling.

Bella laughed and stretched her arms. 'Let's go first thing in the morning.'

'How about 9:30? it's just past the community centre, and no one will be there at that hour.'

The next morning, Bella threw on a loose dress over her bikini. Meanwhile, Elsie spent a good ten minutes wrestling her old bathers over her thighs, hitching them up over her stomach and boob's. The single strap around her neck was a nightmare, but after some struggle, she finally got the clasp to hold. The bright blue swimsuit with an aqua floral pattern had once fitted perfectly. Now? She could hardly breathe, but there was no way she was giving in. She wrapped a beach towel around herself and slipped on her sandals.

The pool was a decent size, and, as expected, they had it to themselves.

'You doing forty laps, Elsie?' Bella asked, giving her a look.

Elsie scoffed. 'No, just paddling around the edge.' She wasn't about to admit that a single lap would probably leave her gasping for air.

Bella dove in, swimming slow but steady to the other end of the pool.

'Wow,' Elsie called out. 'You're fitter than I am!'

'Maybe if your bathers weren't so tight, you'd be able to swim,' Bella teased.

Elsie wasn't one to back down. She pushed off the edge and swam across. She made it barely, but felt quite pleased with herself.

'Try swimming to the other end!' Bella challenged.

Determined, Elsie started a shaky overarm, kicking as

hard as she could. Her head wobbled from side to side as she tried to keep it above water. By the time she reached the halfway mark, exhaustion hit. She grabbed the side of the pool, trying to save face. 'Just doing some kicking,' she called to Bella, unwilling to admit defeat.

She wasn't fooling anyone. Her feet barely made a splash.

'Great exercise,' Elsie lied.

And then, disaster. The strap around her neck gave way.

She felt it snap loose just as the pool doors swung open. In walked four men from the village, all in bathers and sandals, towels draped over their shoulders.

'Morning, ladies,' one of them called. 'Joining us for lap practice?'

'Not today, thanks,' Bella replied with a grin, leaving Elsie to wrestle with her broken strap.

Panic set in. Elsie fumbled, trying to stretch the halter neck strap back around her neck, but it was hopeless. The whole thing came undone, and she was left clutching the fabric against her chest in a desperate attempt to preserve her dignity.

'Psssst! Bella!' Elsie called urgently. 'Get my towel! The strap's broken, and the side is splitting!'

Bella, loved seeing Elsie in a precarious situation, burst out laughing. 'Nope, I'm heading home as soon as I get out.'

'This is no time for joking!' Elsie hissed.

'There's always time for joking,' Bella teased, swimming to the steps and climbing out. She grabbed her towel, threw on her dress, and strolled toward the door without a second glance.

'BELLA! Bella, come back!' Elsie yelled. 'I can't get out like this!'

Bella had left

The men were doing laps, oblivious to her predicament. She calculated how long forty laps would take, far too long. Desperation set in. She had to make a move, but she was at the deep end of the pool.

'Bloody hell, Bella.' Elsie spoke to herself.

Clinging to the side of the pool, Elsie inched toward the shallow end, her bathers barely holding together. Each time she moved, the top slipped, or the side seam ripped a little more. The fabric had completely lost its elasticity, and as water poured in, her bathers stretched further.

By the time she reached the steps, she was a wreck. Taking a deep breath, she bolted out of the pool and reached for her towel.

Except, no towel.

'That bloody Bella.' Elsie said mumbling to herself.

Elsie clutched her bathers to her body with both hands and made a mad dash for the exit, praying she wouldn't run into anyone else.

Just as she reached the doors, Bella jumped out and shouted, 'Boooo!' at the top of her lungs.

Elsie nearly jumped out of her skin.

'Hell, Bella! Where's my towel?!' she yelled, still breathless from fright.

Bella was doubled over with laughter. 'Maybe the men stole it!'

'Bella!' Elsie shrieked. 'Where is it?!'

Bella did a little dance and tossed the towel at her shoulder. 'Got you with the old 'stole your towel' trick! Been wanting to do that for years.'

Elsie groaned and giggled. 'You're impossible, you think

you're so smart,' Elsie shot back, but she was already laughing.

'I am smart! I bought a new pair before we moved here. Two sizes up.'

'Oh, you win,' Elsie admitted.

They walked home, still giggling. By then, Elsie was starting to think Mahjong might've been the better choice after all.

Chapter 15

The village had its fair share of quirky characters, singles, widows, couples, and the migratory types who vanished the moment the weather cooled. Bella preferred her own company, though no one seemed to take the hint. Least of all Keith from number eighteen.

He was pleasant enough, but he had an uncanny knack for roping people into favours they hadn't agreed to.

On her morning walk, just as she passed his unit, the unmistakable creak of Keith's front door stopped her mid-stride.

'Bella!' His voice rang out, far too chipper for someone about to drop a request.

She hesitated. Could she pretend she hadn't heard him?

Too late. He was already jogging toward her, keys jingling in one hand.

'Morning, Keith,' she said, keeping her tone carefully neutral.

'Morning!' He beamed like she'd already agreed to

whatever he was about to ask. 'I was hoping you might do me a favour?'

Her stomach sank. 'What kind of favour?'

Keith wasted no time. 'Could you mind Milly for two weeks while we head off in the van?'

Bella blinked. 'I don't do pet-sitting,' she said quickly, folding her arms. 'I only like horses.'

It wasn't a lie. She didn't like the responsibility, or the guilt. The last time she'd agreed to watch someone's pet, she'd been a kid, minding a friend's budgie. One morning, she'd woken up to find it dead on the cage floor. The friend's mother had screamed at her, accusing her of not feeding it enough. The panic of that moment still hit her in waves whenever someone asked her to care for an animal.

Keith, undeterred, grinned. 'That's perfect! Milly's not a dog or a cat. She's a fish.'

Bella stared at him, lips pressing into a thin line. A fish. How much trouble could a fish really be?

Sensing hesitation, Keith pounced. 'I'll give you a house key. All you have to do is feed her one large pinch of food once a day.'

She frowned. A large pinch. Once a day. It sounded ridiculously simple, but she still didn't like being volunteered.

'Well,' she said slowly, 'if it's just a pinch once a day, I suppose I can manage that.'

Keith's face lit up like he'd won the lottery. 'Oh, thank you, Bella! You're a lifesaver.'

Before she could change her mind, he pressed the keys and the jar of fish food into her hand, thanked her profusely, and jogged back to number eighteen.

Bella stood there, staring at the keys, wondering why she hadn't just said no.

Chapter 16

By the time Bella and Elsie walked into happy hour on Friday night, the room was already buzzing. The familiar hum of chatter mixed with the clinking of glasses, and the unmistakable scent of cheap wine filled the air.

Elsie dug into her pocket, pulling out a five-dollar note, and dropped it into the new money box perched on the table near the door. It had a slot on top and an official looking sticker that seemed far too serious for a casual village gathering.

'That's new,' Bella noted, eyeing the box.

The woman guarding it, a bottle of champagne clutched in one hand, gave a knowing nod. 'You can't be too sure these days.'

Elsie feigned concern. 'Oh? Are there bad types lurking in this village?'

The woman's eyebrows shot up, and she leaned in conspiratorially. 'Well, I've heard there's one with a record.'

Elsie gasped dramatically, placing a hand on her throat.

'Nooo! I'd better start collecting my newspaper earlier before it gets pinched!'

'Do they deliver newspapers here?' the woman asked, suddenly curious.

'You could ask at the office,' Elsie quipped before steering Bella away.

She grinned at her friend. 'You're getting quite the reputation, you know.'

Bella shrugged, long immune to Elsie's antics. Teasing was part of their friendship, a game that made life fun.

Elsie surveyed the room, spotting the same familiar divide: Ted and Annie's group on one side, Dulcie and her friends on the other. The tension between them had been dragging on for weeks, and frankly, it was ridiculous.

Time to fix it.

'Bella, grab that spare chair from Ted's table and move it over to Annie's, would you?'

Bella shot her a suspicious look but obeyed.

Elsie bent down and whispered something to Ted. His face paled, and for a moment, he just stared at her. Then, without argument, he stood up.

'Thanks, Ted,' Elsie said smoothly before turning back to Bella. 'Put this one over there too.'

Bella, catching on, grabbed another chair. Across the room, Annie stood up just as Elsie leaned in and murmured something in her ear. Like Ted, she hesitated, then obeyed.

Elsie stepped back, surveying her work.

'Okay, folks,' she called out, loud enough to hush the room. 'We need to move this table a few feet to the right.'

Surprised faces turned toward her, but no one argued. Chairs screeched against the wooden floor as the two groups, once split, inched closer together.

Elsie rapped her knuckles against the table, making sure

she had their full attention. 'Listen up. We all live on this tiny patch of land in this massive country. No three people should have the power to divide an entire community room. This wedge between you it's uncomfortable, unnecessary, and frankly, childish. So, let's quit the segregation, yes?'

A heavy silence followed, eyes darting away in quiet guilt.

She exhaled. 'Right. Now, grab a chair.' Then, brightening, she added, 'First one to tell a joke gets a free champagne!'

That was the real Elsie ready to fighting for justice in her own strange way. She caught Bella's gaze watching that she didn't go over the top.

'What do you call a lady leaning against a fence?' Joe called out.

Elsie smirked. 'Go on.'

'Eileen!'

A few smiles. No laughter.

'Four out of ten,' Elsie said, shaking her head. 'No champagne for you, Joe.'

Jan spoke up next. 'Did you know there's a lot of AIDS going around in lifestyle villages now?'

A few people looked at her, puzzled. 'No? How?'

She grinned. 'Walking aids, hearing aids, toilet aids!'

Laughter erupted from both sides of the room. The divide, at least for tonight, had dissolved.

'Jan gets a free champagne!' Elsie announced, pleased.

Later, as Bella and Elsie strolled out of the hall, Marion caught up with them. 'That was impressive,' she said. 'You got them back together like a pro.'

Elsie shrugged. 'Learned it in jail. That's how they stop riots.'

Bella choked on a laugh.

Marion blinked, her jaw slightly slack.

Elsie grinned. 'Wouldn't want them to think I have brains. Much more interesting if they believe I'm a jailbird.'

Bella shook her head, still chuckling. 'What did you whisper to Ted and Annie?'

Elsie smirked. 'Told Annie I'd announce exactly how long their affair had been going on. Told Ted I'd call out the last woman he had an affair with. He jumped up so fast, I'm pretty sure one of his exes was sitting at his table.'

Bella let out a loud laugh. 'Straight to the point, huh?'

'Always,' Elsie said, satisfied. 'Solves most problems.'

Chapter 17

A power outage hit the village overnight, and word spread fast. The repair crew estimated another two hours before restoration. With no way to heat water for coffee, Bella took it as a sign from the universe to pour herself and Elsie a morning glass of Pinot Gris.

'Breakfast of champions,' Elsie remarked, setting down a plate of Brie and salted biscuits.

A distant bark cut through their conversation. Elsie tilted her head. 'Wonder whose dog that is?' She took a sip of wine. 'Pets are a nightmare if you ever want to go away. I adore poodles, I've had three, they are such good company. I won't be getting another one, too much hassle. You have to find someone to feed them or pay for a dog hotel.'

Bella nodded absently, her thoughts aligning with Elsie's. Until something jolted her upright.

'Fish! The bloody fish!' she shrieked, nearly toppling her glass as she bolted from her chair.

'What fish?' Elsie called after her, hurrying to keep up.

Bella snatched a single key from the coffee table and grabbed a small plastic jar. 'Keith's!'

'From number eighteen?'

'Yes! I have his key. I was supposed to feed it. The bloody thing even has a name, Milly!'

Fumbling with the lock, Bella heaved a sigh of relief as the door clicked open. The moment they stepped inside, an unpleasant smell wafted toward them.

Elsie wrinkled her nose. 'How long have they been gone?'

'Two weeks,' Bella muttered, her unease growing.

They hurried through the house, scanning for the fish tank. The source of the stench revealed itself halfway down the lounge room wall, a large fish tank with murky grey water motionless and unfiltered.

Elsie squinted. 'Uh-oh.'

Bella's stomach twisted. 'Dead? Is it dead?'

The fish, Milly floated listlessly on top of the water, its fins stiff. The water was stagnant.

'I can't... I just can't touch it,' Bella said, gagging.

'Throw some food near its head,' Elsie suggested, unbothered. 'If it's alive, it'll go for it.'

Bella hesitated, her fingers trembling as she sprinkled flakes onto the water's surface. Nothing.

'What now?' she whispered, panic rising in her stomach.

'Elsie, what now?'

'Down the toilet, I guess. It's the best funeral I can think of.

'Funeral!' The sudden boom of Keith's voice made both women jump. He stood in the doorway, his face twisted in horror.

'Milly?' He pushed past Bella, lunging toward the tank. 'What happened to the water? What happened to MILLY?'

Bella's heart pounded. 'I... I thought she ate yesterday,' she blurted, the lie tumbling out.

Keith ignored her, plunging his hands into the putrid water, his focus entirely on his beloved pet. Lifting Milly's limp body, he cradled her, water dripping onto the carpet. His voice cracked.

'She's gone... she's gone.'

Bella swallowed hard. 'I—I think so too.'

Just then, Keith's wife entered, dragging a suitcase behind her. At the sight of her husband sobbing over the lifeless fish, her expression turned from exhaustion to pure disbelief.

'Milly, Milly! I should never have left you to go on holiday!' Keith wailed, tears streaking his face.

Silently, Elsie slipped away, leaving Bella to endure the fallout alone.

Bella tried to summon a tear. Nothing. 'I'm so sorry. So, so sorry. I was talking to her yesterday!' she grasped desperately.

Keith's head snapped up, his grief sharpening into suspicion. 'I don't think so.' His voice was ice. 'She looks like she's been dead for days. Look how thin she is!'

Bella had no defence. Shame burned in her cheeks.

Keith's wife crossed her arms. 'That's it, Keith. We agreed. No more pets when Milly goes.'

Keith's devastation turned to outrage. 'It's murder!' he howled. 'Murder! She didn't feed Milly properly!'

Bella backed toward the door as an argument erupted behind her.

'Don't be so dramatic,' Keith's wife snapped. 'No more pets. That's final!'

But Keith wasn't letting go. 'Murder!' he bellowed as Bella slipped outside. The fresh air hit her like salvation, but guilt lingered in her chest. She was never taking care of another pet again.

The power was still out. Elsie and Bella were halfway through their second bottle of Pinot Gris when a sharp knock rattled the door.

Bella swung it open to find Keith standing ramrod straight on the doorstep, his arms stiff at his sides like a major general ready to salute. His expression was fierce, his tone even fiercer. 'You are going to replace Milly, or else!'

Bella blinked. 'I'm sorry,' she said, attempting sincerity. 'I'm not good with fish. Only horses.'

Keith's eyes narrowed. 'Tomorrow. A new Milly. Delivered. Or else.'

With that, he spun on his heel and marched off.

Bella barely managed to close the door before collapsing into an exaggerated military march toward the couch. She flopped down, arms swinging, and Elsie joined her in the wildest laughter they'd had in years.

They were still gasping for breath when Elsie's phone rang. She picked it up, giggling.

'Hello?'

A gruff male voice cut in. 'Now, about my car. It's been two weeks, and not even an apology!'

Elsie's eyebrows shot up. Thinking fast, she adopted a terrible accent. 'What u want?'

A pause. Then, suspiciously, 'What?'

'What u want, honey? Wong number!' She jabbed the 'End Call' button and tossed the phone onto the table.

Bella lost it completely. Flat on her back on the couch, she clutched her stomach, one leg waving in the air as she shrieked, 'What does a goldfish take when he's sick?'

Elsie, wiping tears from her eyes, played along. 'What?'

'Vitamin sea!'

'Heavens,' Elsie groaned, 'where did you drag that up from?'

Bella rolled onto her side, still breathless. 'What do you get when you cross a banker with a goldfish?'

'Oh Lord—what?'

'A loan shark!'

That set them both off again.

'No Friday happy hour,' Elsie wheezed, shaking her head.

'No honey toast, and I am never eating fish again!' Bella said through laughter.

Chapter 18

The next day, Elsie wasn't in the mood to stay cooped up at home. Bella, ever the optimist, sensed her restlessness.

'Elsie, how about Mahjong today? It starts at one. We haven't tried it yet. Could be fun,' she suggested brightly.

Elsie sighed, half-amused. 'Better than feeding ducks at the park, I suppose. Alright, let's give it a go.'

The two set off for the community centre, their conversation light and peppered with their usual banter. But as they pushed open the glass doors of the main hall, the lively chatter they had expected was replaced by an eerie silence. The hall was empty.

'No one's here,' Bella murmured, scanning the vacant space.

'They might be in one of the side rooms,' Elsie offered, though her tone lacked confidence.

They ventured down the corridor, peeking through one door after another. At the third, they spotted a group of women hunched over a table, their attention fixed on a cluster of Mahjong tiles.

Elsie tried the handle. The door didn't budge. 'Stuck,' she muttered, giving it another shake.

'Let me,' Bella said with a smirk, stepping forward. 'I'm stronger than you.' But even her efforts couldn't budge the door.

'It's locked,' Bella concluded, rapping on the glass with a polite knock. The women inside didn't so much as glance up.

Elsie's patience snapped. She flattened her hand against the glass and banged hard enough to make it rattle. 'Hey! Can you open the door, please?'

The women remained steadfast in their ignorance, their focus unwavering.

'Are they all deaf?' Elsie hissed, arms crossing tightly over her chest.

'No,' Bella said, her voice tinged with humour. 'They're ignoring us on purpose.'

Elsie's jaw tightened. 'That's not good enough,' she snapped, spinning on her heel and stalking back down the corridor.

'Elsie,' Bella called after her, hurrying to keep up. 'Don't cause a fuss. We can come back later.'

'Not a chance,' Elsie shot back over her shoulder. Elsie really took this to heart, remembering sad times at school when she would be locked out of a game, or locked out of the toilets. Elsie's personality was even then an acquired taste. She didn't think it was acceptable then and she certainly wouldn't accept it at her age.

She remembered one incident where she complained to the teacher and got no support. It was that very day she decided that she had to stick up for herself. No one was coming to save her.

Outside, Elsie shoved past an overgrown bush until she

reached the window to the Mahjong room. Her knuckles rapped against the glass, each knock sharper than the last. One of the women finally looked up, her face a mix of irritation and unease. She whispered something to the others, who huddled closer to their tiles.

'Let us in!' Elsie's voice cut through the glass. 'This window's about to break, and if you don't unlock that door, you'll be paying for it!'

Bella joined in, her tone mock-serious. 'Big trouble if you don't!'

'Big trouble,' Elsie echoed, satisfied with the echo of their united front.

Finally, one of the women, a timid figure who looked like the weakest link stood and shuffled to the door. The lock clicked, and the door swung open with a reluctant creak.

Elsie and Bella strode in, and Elsie wasted no time. 'What's going on here?' she demanded, her voice slicing through the room like a blade.

The sharp featured woman at the table clearly the ringleader gave her a withering look. 'We're playing Mahjong. We always lock the door after everyone is here.'

'Liar!' Elsie's retort cracked like a whip. 'Someone put you up to this. I'm making a formal complaint.'

The ringleader tilted her head, her smile sickly sweet. 'Would you like to join us for a game?'

Elsie's glare could have melted steel. 'No, we'd rather play with scorpions in a bush. You're a horrid lot.'

'Suit yourself,' the woman replied, her smirk unwavering. 'We're in the middle of a game anyway. So you would have to wait.'

Without another word, Elsie grabbed Bella's arm and stormed out.

'Elsie,' Bella panted, struggling to keep up. 'What are you doing now?'

Her answer came as Elsie halted abruptly in front of the large red emergency button mounted on the back wall of the community hall. Without hesitation, she slammed her palm down on it. The siren that followed was deafening, its wail bouncing off every surface.

'That'll bring help faster than a speeding bullet,' Elsie declared, hands on her hips.

Minutes later, Michael, the manager, burst through the back door, his face flushed. 'What's the emergency, Elsie? Bella?' he shouted over the noise.

Elsie waited patiently as he fumbled to silence the alarm. 'Come with us, Mick,' she said firmly.

'It's Michael,' he corrected weakly as she led him back toward the Mahjong room.

Inside, the women were already on their feet, their faces pale and uneasy.

'These women locked us out,' Elsie said, pointing accusingly at the group. 'When we knocked, they ignored us. It's a disgrace, and I want them reprimanded.'

Michael glanced between the two parties, his expression a mix of confusion and exasperation. 'This will be addressed at tonight's community meeting,' he announced. 'Both parties are required to attend.'

As the Mahjong players muttered among themselves, Elsie and Bella exchanged triumphant smiles. That would do, for now.

Chapter 19

The evening buzzed with quiet tension as Mahjong players shuffled into the community centre for the meeting. Elsie claimed a seat near the front, her energy crackling back to life. She wasn't one to let a slight go unanswered, and the Mahjong debacle was far from over.

Michael stood awkwardly at the podium, gripping the edges as if bracing for impact. He tapped his pen to bring the meeting to order. Elsie leaned forward, eyes locked on him like a hawk eyeing its prey. Finally, the moment she'd been waiting for, the lockout was on the agenda.

Michael adjusted his glasses, attempting authority despite the clear reluctance in his voice. 'So, what was your reason for locking the door?' he asked the Mahjong players.

Uneasy silence. Elsie's fingers drummed against the armrest, her patience thinning. Michael repeated the question, already sounding resigned.

The timid woman, the one who had begrudgingly unlocked the door earlier, finally mumbled, 'We don't like them.'

The words landed like a brick being thrown into a still pond.

Elsie's eyes gleamed. There it is. The truth, plain and simple.

Michael frowned, attempting to salvage some dignity. 'Well,' he sighed, 'they probably don't like you either.' He sounded less like an authority figure and more like a weary father caught between squabbling children.

Before Elsie could pounce, another Mahjong player interjected, voice sharp with accusation. 'They have a bad reputation. One of them's a jailbird, and the other's been caught stealing.'

Michael straightened. 'Where's your proof of that?'

'It's well known,' the ringleader said, smirking. 'Everyone in the village knows.'

Elsie shot to her feet, her voice slicing through the room. 'Gossip! We moved here to live, to laugh, to bring some life to this dull place! And yet, you lot treat jokes like mortal sins.'

Michael, rubbing his temples, turned to Elsie and Bella. 'Have either of you been in jail?'

'No,' they answered in unison.

'Have either of you stolen anything or been questioned by the police?'

'No,' they replied, deadpan.

Michael exhaled. 'Then where did this gossip come from?'

Silence. A few Mahjong players suddenly found their shoelaces fascinating.

Elsie seized the moment. 'It came from me,' she declared, unapologetic. 'I say funny things to get a laugh, to lighten the mood. But you lot,' she gestured at them dramatically, 'have forgotten how to laugh.'

Michael sighed, his patience threadbare. 'Elsie you are definitely not subtle and people can easily take offence. What else do you have against Elsie and Bella?'

A bold woman piped up. 'They're after our husbands.'

Elsie blinked, then burst into laughter so sudden it startled Bella, who joined in, clutching her side.

'Bloody hell!' Elsie gasped, wiping a tear from her eye. 'Have you had a good look at your husbands lately? They're as old and worn out as the shag carpet in your great aunt's hallway!'

Bella, barely breathing through laughter, added, 'And their hearing's as dead as their sense of humour!'

Michael fought to keep a straight face. 'Who exactly are they targeting as future boyfriends?'

'None,' Elsie snorted. 'But if you're so worried, wrap those handsome devils in cotton wool and leave them at home. Bella and I won't come to any more community events. Instead, we'll start doing drugs and throwing wild parties at our place. Cars pulling up all hours, neon lights, maybe even a bouncer at the door.'

Michael inhaled sharply. 'Elsie please backoff, are you into drugs?'

'Of course not,' she replied, feigning outrage. 'But I hear it's extremely lucrative. I've never even smoked, and neither has Bella. Right, Bella?'

'Right,' Bella confirmed, still giggling.

Elsie's grin turned wicked. 'But let's be fair here, how many of you Mahjong players have done drugs?'

Three hands hesitantly rose.

Elsie arched an eyebrow. 'Well, well, isn't that telling?' She leaned back. 'How many of you have been married more than once?'

A few more hands crept up.

'There we go,' Elsie said smugly. 'With a little more digging, we'd have a river of secrets pouring out.'

Bella, still chuckling, added, 'Ever hear of people in glass houses?'

Michael, utterly done, rubbed his face. 'Grow up, all of you. This is ridiculous. Apologise before you leave.'

Grumbling apologies were exchanged as the meeting adjourned. As Michael, Elsie, and Bella walked toward the main entrance, he turned to Elsie with caution. 'By the way, Elsie... please don't ring the emergency bell again.'

Elsie's steps stopped. 'Why not?' she asked, feigning innocence.

Michael sighed. 'There's a record kept of every time it's rung. We have to log the details and file a report. I'm up for a company award for best village manager, and it might look bad if it's overused.'

Elsie stopped in her tracks, turned to him with mock outrage, then turned again, this time heading for the back wall where the big red emergency button gleamed.

Michael's eyes widened. 'Elsie, don't you da...'

Too late.

Elsie slammed her palm against the button.

The siren wailed, its sound bouncing off the walls.

Michael scrambled to silence it, nearly dropping the control panel. 'What the '

'Don't be a wimp, Mick,' Elsie said, hands on her hips. 'I live here, and I'll press that button whenever I see fit. Go read your company brochure. Community Security, page twenty-three. It's for resident safety... or was that just a sales pitch, Mick?'

Michael muttered something about checking the brochure later as he fumbled with the controls.

One thing he knew for certain, the village was never dull.

Chapter 20

Elsie was still lost in thought over the Mahjong debacle, mentally plotting ways to smooth things over and reclaim the goodwill of their neighbours. The silence was broken by Bella's sudden burst of inspiration.

'What if we throw a fancy-dress night?'

Elsie's face brightened. 'That's a solid idea! Should we pick a theme?'

Bella tapped a finger against her chin. 'Something fun. Maybe an Addams Family night? Or Rocky Horror?'

Elsie shook her head, chuckling. 'Put it to a vote, and we'll end up with something dull like a teddy bears' picnic.'

Bella snorted. 'True.'

After tossing ideas back and forth, they landed on an Egyptian-themed night. With a plan in motion, Elsie got to work, scribbling invitations and designing a bold poster for the community hall's message board. Excitement fizzed between them as they fine-tuned the details.

Delivering the invitations turned into an adventure of its own. They meandered through the village, knocking on doors and chatting with the locals. Some responded with indifference, while others bombarded them with costume ideas. Bella had already decided on Cleopatra. When she mentioned it, Elsie admitted she'd been considering the same.

'I'll think of something else,' Elsie said, a glint of mischief in her eye.

Bella narrowed hers. 'That worries me.'

The week flew by in a flurry of preparations. One afternoon, they headed to the shopping centre for final costume pieces. Bella immediately zeroed in on a sleek black wig, perfect for her Cleopatra transformation.

'I'll meet you at the coffee shop,' Elsie called over her shoulder before disappearing into another aisle.

Later, as Elsie returned to the coffee shop, Bella frowned when she saw the mountain of supplies Elsie had bought.

'Got everything you need?'

'Absolutely!' Elsie grinned. The top of one bag over-flowed with toilet paper.

Bella smirked. 'Big sale on toilet paper, was there?'

'Huge. I'm stocked up for months.'

Chapter 21

At last, the big night arrived. Bella meticulously assembled her Cleopatra look, an old white sheet transformed into a flowing gown, layered necklaces, long earrings, and the perfect black wig styled into a sharp bob. With dramatic eyeliner accentuating her eyes, she admired her regal transformation before heading out to collect Elsie.

Excitement buzzed in her chest as she knocked on Elsie's door.

No answer.

She frowned and knocked again. Still nothing.

Testing the handle, she found it locked. Confusion flickered into disappointment.

Surely Elsie hadn't gone without her?

The community room buzzed with life as guests poured in, draped in vibrant Egyptian costumes. At the centre stood Alf, the self-appointed Master of Ceremonies, proudly wearing a makeshift Pharaoh's headdress a striped tea towel tied with a dark gold ribbon from Christmas wrapping. He clapped his hands, calling for attention.

'Alright, let's see who the best Cleopatra is!' he announced, his voice cutting through the cheerful chatter.

Five Cleopatras emerged from the crowd, each flaunting their elaborate outfits. Alf squinted, tapping his chin in mock deliberation. 'This is tough. You all look so exotic!'

One contender seized the moment, sauntering forward with a slow, theatrical sway. Gasps rippled through the room as she reached into her bodice and pulled out a long, plastic snake. With a playful shimmy, she twirled it around her arms before draping it over Alf's shoulders.

The room erupted in laughter and applause.

'Well, that settles it!' Alf declared, barely suppressing a grin. 'Number four, you're the winner! The snake tipped the scales.'

Amid cries of 'rigged!' and 'not fair!', the snake-wielding Cleopatra accepted her box of chocolates, curtsying with exaggerated grace.

After a break for snacks and champagne, Alf moved on to the next round: most unusual costume. A colourful mix of contestants stepped forward, priests, snake charmers, and, oddly, a jester in full harlequin attire.

Alf frowned. 'Jester, what are you doing here?'

The jester shrugged. 'Only costume I own.'

Before Alf could respond, a strange, high-pitched squeaking noise filled the room, like an old hinge in desperate need of oil. Heads turned as it grew louder.

'Where's that coming from?' someone muttered.

Syd, a golfer, pointed toward a stack of cardboard boxes against the far wall. 'Over there!'

Alf approached cautiously. The squeaking intensified.

'It's time I rise!' a quivering voice boomed from within the boxes. Gasps and giggles rippled through the crowd.

Alf hesitated. 'What on earth?' He tugged at the top box.

The male voice thundered again. 'Help me reappear! I've been trapped for thousands of years!'

The crowd pressed closer, buzzing with anticipation. Alf removed the top layer of cardboard, and with a dramatic rustle, a figure slowly began to sit up. Alf held out his hand to help. It was a mummy, wrapped head to toe in white.

'I rise!' it declared, swaying slightly.

Alf kept helping the mummy to its feet. The room fell silent.

'Unwrap me!' the male voice commanded.

Alf hesitated, but the crowd, now fully invested, egged him on. He pulled at the endless layers of white, unraveling strip after strip until bare legs emerged. Then feet. Then finally Elsie.

Standing proudly in a new swimsuit, surrounded by piles of toilet paper. The room exploded with laughter. Someone handed her a glass of champagne, which she accepted with a mock curtsy.

'That was brilliant!' Bella exclaimed, wiping tears from her eyes.

The crowd peppered Elsie with questions. 'How did you do all this? How did you get a male voice?' She waved them off with a cheeky grin. 'Old Egyptian secret,' she laughingly replied.

Later, as the festivities wound down, Elsie and Bella strolled home, an overcoat draped over Elsie's swimsuit. They settled in with a pot of tea and chocolate coated teddy bear biscuits, still giggling.

'How did you pull that off?' Bella asked, shaking her head in disbelief.

Elsie grinned. 'Took some teamwork. Emma and the twins wrapped me up and stashed me in the boxes earlier. Took forever, but it was worth it.'

'Oh, and that voice?' Bella questioned further.

'Sam and Stacey recorded it on my phone. Left space between lines so I could time it right. Think they got the hinges squeaking from a horror movie. Clever pair, those two.'

Bella smirked. 'Oh, I noticed something else, you have new bathers.

Elsie sighed dramatically. 'Busted.'

'What size, Elsie?'

'Not telling, but let's just say a lot bigger than my old ones.'

Bella snorted. 'They'd need to be!'

Elsie pouted. 'I didn't even get any chocolates.'

Bella laughed. 'I didn't win best Cleopatra either, it took me forever to do my eyeliner!'

Elsie sighed. 'That snake charming Cleopatra had us beat. Wish I'd thought of it first.'

Bella burst into laughter. 'You certainly stole the show. Almost nude, and still the star of the night!'

Elsie winked. 'Not bad for a mummy wrapped in toilet paper.'

Chapter 22

The late-morning sun streamed into Bella's courtyard as she and Elsie enjoyed a pot of tea together. Their laughter occasionally punctuating the tranquil air.

'What'll we do today?' Bella mused, stirring her cup.

'Time to try something new?' Elsie suggested.

'Good idea. What do you have in mind?' Bella asked. 'Stir up the village by running through it stark naked?'

Elsie choked on her tea.

Bella smirked. 'I'll stop short of daring you though, after letting everyone see you in bathers.'

'You're right,' Elsie said. 'I'm better at winning money. Let's try Bingo. We can split whatever I win.'

Bella inclined her head. 'What if I win? That could easily happen, you know.'

Elsie grinned. 'Oh, Bella, we both know I have a higher win rate than you. When's the last time you won anything?'

Bella sat back, smug. 'Funny, I don't remember you winning either.'

'Convenient,' Elsie shot back.

'Actually, I won $15.00 once.'

'Was it a joint ticket or one of your own?'

'Mine,' Bella said proudly.

Elsie leaned in. 'And how on earth did you manage to spend all that money by yourself?'

Bella shrugged. 'Bought another ticket. Didn't do any good.'

Elsie laughed. 'Typical.'

'Ever been to the horse races?' Bella asked.

'No,' Elsie admitted. 'but it's still on my bucket list.'

Later that morning, they walked to the village office to collect their mail. Elsie paused, frowning. 'Have you ever noticed we don't have letterboxes at our units? Saves the village money and makes sure we get a daily walk. Sneaky, don't you think?'

Bella shrugged. 'I don't mind the walk. If we want mail, that's the deal.'

Elsie smirked. 'It's not about the mail, it's the principle.'

A few days later, Bella knocked on Elsie's door and walked in, as usual.

'Good morning, Elsie. Get dressed we're going shopping.'

Elsie, still in her nightie and dressing gown, sipped her tea. 'Shopping? What for?'

Bella folded her arms. 'A bucket list is no good unless you start crossing things off.'

Elsie squinted. 'What things?'

'We need sophisticated outfits we're going to the Melbourne Cup.'

Elsie's face lit up. 'The races? The Melbourne Cup?' She clutched her teacup. 'That's exciting! When did you come up with that idea?'

'Last week, when you were mentioned you had never

gone to a race meeting. I thought, 'I'm not listening to this nonsense for the next five years.' So, I booked a taxi to go shopping for our outfits. It'll be here in twenty minutes.'

Elsie blinked. 'Lucky I don't have any plans today.'

'You don't,' Bella said.

Elsie glanced toward her wardrobe. 'I might have something tucked away…'

'No, you don't,' Bella interrupted. 'You threw out all your old glad rags before we moved. So, I know for a fact that you have nothing suitable.'

THE TAXI DROPPED them off in Bourke Street, right in the heart of the city's shopping district.

'I didn't bring any shopping bags,' Elsie said.

Bella sighed. 'Oh, for heaven's sake, Elsie. We're going upmarket, not buying bread and milk.'

The streets bustled with office workers clutching takeaway coffees, moving in synchronised chaos without colliding. The air buzzed with city energy.

'Let's grab a coffee first,' Bella suggested.

They ducked into a cozy café, ordering a cappuccino and a hot chocolate.

'This is nice,' Elsie said, settling into her chair.

Bella sipped her coffee. 'So, about this horse racing business you've never actually been before, have you?'

'No, but I've always been lucky with the horses.'

Bella smirked. 'That's a fib.'

'It is not!' Elsie protested. 'I used to win all the time in the Melbourne Cup sweep. The neighbours would put money in, we'd draw horses, and the lucky ones took home the prize.'

Bella shook her head. 'Oh, you can stretch a story.'

'I'm serious!' Elsie said. 'Dad even knew a jockey, he met him at the pub. He used to bet on whatever horse the guy was riding. Mind you, some of those nags are probably still running, they were so slow.'

Bella chuckled, standing up. 'All right, storyteller. Time to shop.'

Elsie drained her cup, grinning. Her bucket list was finally coming to life.

Chapter 23

They stepped into the throng of office workers, the crowd moving like a choreographed dance. Coffee cups in hand, not a single collision in sight. The city hummed with energy.

The entrance to David Jones was packed, barely any room to squeeze inside. Fortunately, Bella, being taller, could see the best way through. She took the lead, weaving through the crowd until they reached the escalator.

'Isn't this fun?' Bella said as they glided upward. 'I wonder what fashion colours are in this season?'

At the top, they were greeted by an enormous display of shoes. Both paused to admire them before agreeing they'd come back for footwear once their outfits were sorted.

'Up we go again!' Elsie grinned. 'I feel like it's Christmas.'

'It will be when I see you parting with your cash,' Bella teased.

Finally, they reached the fashion level. Elsie's eyes lit up as she spotted a display. 'Oh, look at that dress!'

Draped elegantly on a mannequin was a stunning, slim-fitting, sparkling blue gown the kind of dress that belonged in a fairy tale, worn by someone about to waltz at a grand ball.

'Mmm, definitely more me than you. I think I'll try it on,' Bella declared.

'I saw it first!' Elsie huffed.

Bella smirked. 'You're a little lumpy for that style.'

'Lumpy?! That's a bit harsh, Bella!'

'The truth always hurts,' Bella chuckled.

Elsie folded her arms. 'I gave up dieting because I didn't want to look like a stick.'

'What century were you ever on a diet?' Bella shot back. 'Watch out, or you'll be next for the dementia test.'

They continued browsing the racks of elegant evening gowns, chatting about colours and styles.

'I think I'll look for something in lilac or mauve,' Bella mused.

'Good idea,' Elsie agreed. 'Then we can put some lilac rinse through your greys to match.'

'I don't think so,' Bella said flatly.

'What colour are you thinking, Elsie?'

'I don't know until I see it. That's how I shop I see it, I love it, I buy it.'

Bella sighed. 'I think this department is a little too formal for us. It's a day at the races, not a royal ball.'

'True,' Elsie admitted. 'But it's nice to dream, isn't it?'

They wandered deeper into the department, where floral, summery dresses took centre stage. Elsie admired the suits and kaftans, running her fingers over the light, airy fabrics.

'Look at this, Elsie!' Bella called.

Elsie walked over to see Bella staring at a breathtaking

violet dress. It had a V-neckline, short sheer sleeves, and a cinched waist that promised a flattering silhouette.

'Bella, this has your name written all over it. It's gorgeous!'

'Oh, it really does,' Bella murmured, plucking it off the rack and heading for the fitting room.

Elsie waited outside. When Bella finally emerged, Elsie let out an ear-piercing wolf whistle.

'That's a perfect fit, Bella!'

Bella admired herself in the mirror, turning this way and that. 'I'll pair it with a black bag and shoes…'

'Good choice,' Elsie nodded. 'But I still think violet in your hair would be a bit much.'

Bella rolled her eyes. 'I was never going to put violet in my greys, Elsie. That was one of your giddy ideas.'

'Shame,' Elsie smirked. 'But that dress is divine. It makes you look about sixty.'

Bella groaned. 'Just spoil the moment, why don't you? I looked sixty before I put it on now I look fifty.'

'Dream on,' Elsie snorted.

Chapter 24

'Watch out, here comes the salesgirl. She'll tell you how beautiful you look get ready for it, and don't believe a word,' Elsie whispered.

They barely stifled their laughter as the young salesgirl approached with a bright smile. 'That looks beautiful! It's so flattering and makes you look so young.'

Elsie whispered. 'Told you. Can't trust 'em.'

Bella shook her head, amused. 'It's perfect for the races.'

'Absolutely,' the salesgirl chirped. 'You just need a hat to go with it.'

Bella's eyes widened. 'Elsie, we forgot about the hats! Oh, hell's bells, we might be shopping for weeks.'

The salesgirl turned to Elsie. 'And what are you looking for today?'

Elsie sighed dramatically. 'Something that will make me look fifty as well.'

'We have that same dress in other colours if you'd like to try them on,' the salesgirl suggested eagerly.

Elsie rolled her eyes. 'I think we're past the dress alike stage. That was cute when we were fourteen.' She wandered off, leaving Bella chuckling.

It wasn't long before Elsie reappeared in the dressing room with two dresses: a navy blue lace number and a kaftan. While Bella was distracted at another rack, Elsie snuck up behind her.

'Found it,' she said loudly.

Bella turned and burst out laughing.

Elsie stood there, nearly swallowed by a multicoloured kaftan, the fabric pooling at her feet like a collapsed tent. She looked like a floating blimp.

'That looks beautiful on you,' the salesgirl gushed.

'Not really, it's a joke.' Elsie spluttered, heading back to the change rooms.

A moment later, Bella spotted a pale blue skirt and matching top that seemed perfect for Elsie. Holding it up, she called, 'Found this, Elsie! I think it'll suit you better than the kaftan.'

The outfit had a rounded neckline, capped sleeves, and a beautifully full skirt. Elsie's face lit up the moment she saw it. 'Love the colour, Bella.'

When she stepped out of the dressing room, she called Bella in for approval. 'At least I won't have to endure another, that looks beautiful, you look so young' from the salesgirl.'

Bella grinned. 'This outfit is a winner.'

With their outfits sorted, they left the clothing floor behind and made their way to the shoe department.

'Maybe we should come back next week for shoes,' Elsie suggested, shifting a few shopping bags to her other arm.

Bella shook her head. 'No, the Cup's on Tuesday. We don't have time for another shopping trip.'

As Bella scanned the shelves she chose a pair of sleek black shoes. They were shiny patent leather with a low heel, stylish yet comfortable. A matching handbag sat nearby, as if waiting for her. 'Perfect,' she declared, turning to the saleslady. 'I'll take these.'

'Great choice,' the woman said as she led Bella to the register.

'Lucky to get the exact bag to match,' Bella mused, feeling satisfied. 'One more thing to tick off the list. Now, just the hat to go.'

Meanwhile, Elsie had settled onto a low display box, feet propped in front of a floor mirror. She let out a delighted gasp. 'Oh, Bella, I love these!'

Bella glanced over. 'The heels are so high,' she remarked.

Elsie, completely undeterred, took a few slow steps, then another lap around the store.

'Do they fit well?' Bella asked.

'Perfectly,' Elsie beamed.

Bella crossed her arms. 'High heels at our age are a risk, especially when we might be walking on grass.'

Elsie stopped mid-stride. 'Grass? I thought we'd be in the members' dining room.'

Bella answered with a questioning look on her face. 'We will be, but there's no guarantee we won't walk on some grass. Those heels aren't exactly 'race day practical.'

'I'll wear them around the house first to break them in,' Elsie countered.

Bella smirked. 'Well, you've got four days. Better start now. Just remember, when your feet start screaming, I warned you.'

'Fiddle-sticks!' Elsie scoffed. 'They're my size. What could go wrong?'

With that, she marched to the register, buying her beloved black stilettos and a bag to match.

After a well-earned break over coffee and sandwiches, they regained their energy for the final stretch.

'Hats next,' Bella said, determined.

'Ground floor,' Elsie nodded.

As they stepped into the accessories section, Elsie sighed. 'Hats look ridiculous on me. My head is way too big.'

'I suit hats perfectly,' Bella replied with a smug smile. 'I did a modelling course when I was eighteen. They told me I could have been a hat model.'

Elsie shot her a look. 'You're full of it today, Bella.'

'I used to have a few fancy hats for weddings,' Elsie continued.

Bella shook her head. 'That was about a hundred years ago. No one wears hats to weddings anymore. Just the races. But the Cup is different it's a once a year show off day. Everyone loves dressing up. You'll see on Tuesday. You're going to love it.'

Elsie followed Bella toward the hat display.

Bella found a small fascinator with a round base and three violet feathers off to the side, an elegant match for her dress. Elsie, on the other hand, opted for a wide brimmed straw hat, adorned with blue and white daisies around the headband.

'We don't need any more bags to carry,' Elsie groaned. 'We look like we've bought the entire store.'

Laughing, they hailed a taxi, squeezing their overflowing shopping bags between them in the back seat, as they left the city behind.

Chapter 25

Elsie practically bounced on her feet. 'I'm so excited to finally be going to the Melbourne Cup! It's the oldest horse race in Australia.'

Bella, ever composed, gave a knowing nod. 'I've been before, of course.'

Elsie smirked. 'Of course, you have way back in the 1920s.'

Determined to break in her new black high heels before race day, Elsie insisted on wearing them everywhere. As they strolled up the driveway to collect the mail, she felt a sharp pinch at the back of her left foot.

'Bit sore on the heel,' Elsie admitted, shifting uncomfortably.

'I put socks on with mine last night, and they're stretched just right today,' Bella offered. 'Why don't you try that?'

'Thanks, Bella. Elsie agreed. 'I'll give it a go when I get home.'

Back inside, Elsie took the advice and stuffed her feet

now wrapped in thick socks into the stubborn heels. Strutting next door to Bella's unit, she threw out her arms. 'What do you think?'

Bella gave an approving nod. 'That's the idea. A couple of hours, and they'll be as right as rain.'

Elsie chose not to mention the blisters already forming. Surely, they'd heal before Tuesday.

'I'm going to bingo this afternoon,' Bella said. 'Want to come?'

'Yes, but I'll have to keep the high heels on.' Elsie replied.

'That's fine. No one will notice or they'll think you've got a hot date after bingo.'

At the community hall, Elsie's heels clacked loudly on the polished floor. She ignored the odd looks her socks and stilettos combo earned, instead scanning for a place to sit. Spotting the golfing clique, she waved with exaggerated enthusiasm.

'Mind if we sit here?' Elsie asked, making refusal awkward.

'Yes, that's fine,' said golfing Jan.

A nosy golfer leaned in. 'Are you going out after bingo?'

'Yes. Hot date,' Elsie replied.

'Anyone we know?' another voice chimed in.

Elsie grinned. 'Not telling. But not a golfer, that's for sure. 'Hole in one' and 'birdie' just aren't words that do it for me.'

The bingo caller, Robert, took his place at the front. His voice boomed through the hall. 'Is everyone ready to start? Cards on the table, eyes down.'

'Oh, what a loud, sexy voice,' Elsie remarked, loud enough for the table to hear.

Bella leaned toward her. 'That's his wife sitting next to you.'

Elsie turned and beamed at Beryl, who pursed her lips but said nothing.

'Legs 11!' Robert called.

'I've got that!' Elsie yelled, waving her card.

'No, you don't,' Bella hissed.

Elsie glanced down. 'Oh, my mistake. Just waiting for the fun to start.'

Beryl, ever composed, leaned in with a tight smile. 'Don't worry, dearie, you'll get some numbers soon. Just be patient.'

Elsie studied her, taking in the too tight twinset, mismatched scarf, and slightly askew hat. 'Pardon, dearie?' she replied, the sarcasm thick.

'I'm just trying to teach you patience with bingo,' Beryl said sweetly.

Elsie tilted her head. 'Knock, knock.'

Beryl hesitated, then humoured her. 'Who's there?'

'Boo.'

'Boo who?'

'I'd cry too if I played bingo like you.'

A collective gasp rippled through the table.

'Oh, you're trying to be funny, dearie,' Beryl said with a forced smile.

Bella shifted uncomfortably in her seat but wisely stayed out of it.

The game dragged on. Elsie's patience wore thin.

'Thirty-five, jump and jive!' Robert called.

Elsie sighed dramatically. 'I don't have that either.'

Bella stifled a laugh. 'You and Beryl missed forty-four, 'close the door,' and fifty-four, 'clean the floor.''

Elsie groaned. 'I'm already over this.' Her feet

throbbed, her bingo card was depressingly empty, and if one more person called her 'dearie,' she might lose it entirely.

'Bingo isn't as entertaining as a strip show, is it, Bella?'

Bella smirked. 'No, but you are, dearie.'

Elsie rolled her eyes. 'Excuse me, Beryl, is there any booze here at bingo?'

Beryl looked scandalised. 'Oh no, it's a wholesome, fun gathering. We have champagne at drinks on Friday night, though.'

Elsie scoffed. 'Regulated, is it? Mmm. I have a whole bottle of whiskey at night.'

Beryl's eyes widened in horror. 'Oh, my goodness!'

Elsie shrugged. 'Yep. I sleep so well.'

Beryl leaned in with a panicked smile, eyes glinting with Mother Teresa level concern. 'Elsie, I have a friend whose husband goes to Alcoholics Anonymous. Would you like me to get you the phone number?'

Elsie patted her hand. 'Don't bother, sweetie. You're a dear, but I'm beyond saving.'

With that, Elsie stood, tapping Bella on the shoulder. 'My feet are killing me, and I have to get ready for my hot date. Are you staying for another game?'

Bella chuckled. 'I'll walk back with you, dearie. You've already had way too much to drink today.'

As they walked home, Elsie grumbled, 'You know I hate being called 'dearie' or 'sweetie.' It makes me sound like an insipid old lady in a straitjacket.'

Bella grinned. 'Oh dearie, I would never have guessed.'

Elsie let out an exasperated sigh. 'OMG. Bingo is definitely not for me. I'm much luckier at picking winning horses. Just wait till Tuesday you'll see.'

Chapter 26

The road back to their units stretched a neat 400 meters, a bitumen strip flanked by narrow lawns. Each house had its own personality scattered plants, carefully trimmed hedges, and clusters of kitschy statues that seemed to guard the fronts like silent sentinels.

Elsie paused halfway, bending to take off her high heels. 'I'm sure my heel is bleeding, Bella. What a silly idea to buy high heels. You shouldn't have suggested it.'

Bella snorted. 'Me? Ha! You don't need me to get into trouble. What was with that *Knock, Knock* joke? Poor Beryl didn't even realise you hated being called 'dearie.'

Elsie stepped onto the soft grass in her socks, avoiding the shrubs and garden ornaments. 'And about that whiskey,' Bella continued, 'if the bingo ladies didn't already think we're criminals, now they'll be convinced you're an alcoholic.'

They both burst into laughter. Bella gave Elsie a playful nudge in the side, sending her stumbling. Her foot caught on a concrete statue of Snow White, and Elsie toppled over.

The seven dwarfs arranged in a neat line tumbled into disarray as Elsie landed squarely on them. The edges of the concrete dwarfs dug into her feet, and legs as she fell on the grass.

'OWW, OWW! My foot!' Elsie cried out. She was sprawled on the grass and reaching for her injured foot. She struggled momentarily trying to hold back tears of shock that had pooled in her eyes.

'Here,' Bella said, stifling a laugh. 'Put your arms around my waist. I'll steady you.'

Elsie tried to sit up, but the dwarfs seemed to have joined forces with her clothes, refusing to let her move. A sharp pain in her foot demanded all her attention.

Hearing the commotion, the front door of the nearest unit flew open. Lorna and Joe appeared, curiosity plastered across their faces.

'What's going on out here?' Joe called, peering at the scene.

'Elsie's had a fall,' Bella said, waving him over.

Joe disappeared back inside as Lorna carefully approached, looking concerned. 'What happened?'

'Bloody Snow White got me!' Elsie hollered. 'And the seven dwarfs were in on it too!'

Lorna's eyes widened. The absurdity of the statement left her momentarily speechless. Joe with his big white beard returned, pushing a walker ahead of him.

'This'll do the trick,' he said confidently, setting it near Elsie. 'Hold onto the handles and get up on your good foot...'

Joe stopped mid-sentence, staring at Elsie's sock clad feet. 'Heavens above, where are your shoes? You shouldn't be outside without proper footwear!'

'Save it, Santa,' Elsie snapped.

Bella held up the shoes, wincing. 'I've got them.'

Joe shook his head, his tone turning lecturing. 'See? This is why you wear proper footwear!' Outside in just socks! Didn't you learn better when you were young?'

Elsie, still tangled in the dwarfs, screamed her response. 'I've got Cherokee blood. It's in my nature to avoid shoes.'

A combined effort finally got Elsie upright and seated on the walker. She was panting, too tired to argue for the moment. Joe patted her back. 'Now rest. A fall can be dangerous at your age. Bella, why don't you fetch her walker from her unit?'

Elsie stiffened. 'I do not have a bloody walker, and I do not need one.' she bellowed. 'It's just the excitement of the Melbourne Cup and bingo, all in one day!'

Joe recoiled, muttering, 'Odd.' He glanced at Lorna, shaking his head. 'Shoes. She should've known better.'

Bella knelt to inspect Elsie's foot. 'It's swollen. Really swollen. This might be a broken bone. We'd better call an ambulance.'

'An ambulance!' Elsie groaned. 'Why is everyone always trying to put me in a box?'

'I'll put you in one myself if you don't stop screaming,' Bella retorted.

Elsie leaned back, grimacing. 'Bella, did you bring your whiskey flask? I could do with a shot.'

'No! Absolutely not!' Joe barked. 'Not before the ambulance gets here to assess you.'

'It's already assessed,' Elsie snapped. 'I'm in bloody pain!'

The ambulance arrived, Joe directing the paramedics like a field marshal. Elsie barely noticed his attempts to help, muttering to Bella, 'He's got mid level manager syndrome just loves telling people what to do.'

'Like someone else I know.' Bella said.

Once inside the ambulance, the medics administered a sedative, finally settling Elsie's protests.

At the hospital, Elsie waited for the X-rays, by chatting up the staff. When the doctor arrived, she greeted him with a narrowed glare.

'Nothing broken,' he announced after glancing at the results. 'Just sprained ligaments. You'll need to rest it, elevate your leg, and avoid putting any weight on it for four to six weeks. Probably need a wheelchair for a few weeks.'

He reached for a cast. 'I'll plaster it to keep it immobile.'

Elsie balked. 'I'm not using a bloody wheelchair. I have tickets to the Melbourne Cup on Tuesday, and my new outfit isn't wheelchair friendly!'

The doctor raised an amused eyebrow. 'Feisty.'

'Yes, and stop talking to me like I'm feeble,' she shot back. 'Next, you'll be asking me to count backward from one hundred by sevens.'

The doctor laughed. 'How about this? I'll recommend a knee walker, like a scooter. You'll stay mobile and still make it to the Cup.'

'Thank you!' Elsie said, mollified. 'At least you're not telling me *Knock, Knock* jokes. So childish.'

He chuckled as he worked on her cast. 'Looks like you've got blisters from those heels. Separate incident?'

'Trying to keep up with fashion is deadly,' she replied.

After regaling him with stories from the retirement village, she was finally fitted for the scooter.

'All done,' the doctor said. 'Rest up. Keep your ankle elevated. Check back in four weeks, and we will see how it is.'

Elsie eyed the knee walker critically. 'I hope this is a top of the line model. I'm going to the Melbourne Cup remember, and it had better not ruin my look.'

'It's definitely more upmarket than a wheelchair,' the doctor quipped.

Elsie grinned. 'Fine. This better be the turbo mode!

Chapter 27

The sound of Elsie's knee scooter wheels clicking against the tiled entryway filled the air as Bella ushered her toward the waiting taxi.

'Come on, Elsie, the taxi's here!' Bella called over her shoulder.

Elsie maneuverer her contraption down the step with precision honed over weeks of practice. 'I'm going as fast as I can, Bella! You're lucky I didn't insist on a red carpet roll-out,' she quipped.

Despite Bella's suggestion to skip the Melbourne Cup this year, Elsie had countered with an impassioned argument about life's unpredictability and the futility of letting good outfits go unworn. Bella, accustomed to Elsie's flair for dramatics, had surrendered.

The taxi driver's expression soured as soon as he saw the knee walker. 'You should've booked a wheelchair taxi,' he grumbled, clearly unimpressed.

'I'm not arriving at my first Melbourne Cup in a maxi taxi!' Elsie snapped, her voice rising enough to make the driver wince. Reluctantly, he loaded the knee scooter into the trunk, muttering about the inconvenience as he slammed the lid.

'Main gate,' Bella instructed.

The ride began in terse silence, but soon the driver softened, glancing at the pair in the rearview mirror. 'You ladies look sharp. First Cup for either of you?'

'Her first,' Bella said, smiling.

'Well, good luck! I've got my money on Further North,' the driver said conspiratorially, his insider tone offset by a dramatic wink caught in the rear view mirror. Bella, unimpressed by the tip, jotted it down anyway, circling the name with her glittery violet pen.

When they arrived at Flemington Racecourse, Elsie paused to admire the sprawling displays of floribunda roses. The brilliant yellow blooms seemed to shout celebration, framing the bustling crowds with a festive border.

Inside, the spectacle was mesmerising. The eclectic parade of fashions left Elsie giddy with ad studded creations, it was a feast of whimsy and elegance. Men strutted in tailored suits or outrageous novelty outfits, while women teetered on heels in skimpy summer dresses.

'Oh, Bella, it's even better than I imagined! Look at those suits horses and jockeys all over them!' Elsie pointed to a group of six men in matching yellow ensembles. 'They win!'

Bella decided to immortalise the moment with her new iPhone.

'Go stand with them, Elsie,' she urged.

Elsie scooted over, waving at the men. 'Excuse me, gentlemen, I'm a reporter for the Insane Madness Press for the Elderly. Mind if I join you for a photo?'

The men, already several drinks in, roared with

laughter and pulled her into their midst. Bella, fumbling with her phone, managed to snap the shot just as one man declared his pick for the race: 'Forever Young!'

Elsie wheeled away, delighted by the chaos. 'Bella, I'm coming every year from now on,' she announced.

As the day unfolded, the champagne flowed, and the antics grew more entertaining. Bella spotted a woman in a sheer mini dress struggling across the grass, her heels sinking into the ground with each step. When one shoe stuck, the inevitable tumble sent the woman into hysterics, her mini skirt leaving little to the imagination.

'Glad that's not me,' Bella chuckled.

Elsie, undeterred by any mishaps, found herself caught in one of her own. Following Bella toward the fashion parade, she accidentally rolled up a ramp and straight through a group of impeccably dressed women.

'This way,' a woman in pink gestured, stepping aside to let Elsie pass.

Focused on the stunning floral wall display, Elsie didn't realise Bella was no longer in front of her. She pushed the knee walker along, mumbling, 'Ramps are great,' expecting Bella to respond. Instead, she found herself at the entrance of a grand stage.

'Our next entrant is...' the announcer's voice boomed through the speakers.

Elsie barely had time to react before she crossed a threshold, rolling onto the red carpet. Flashbulbs erupted. Applause rang out. From the audience. Bella was at the edge of the audience, doubled over, tears streaming down her face. 'Wrong path, Elsie!' she howled.

The male announcer flipped through his notes. 'I can't find this one's name...' he whispered into the mic. Then, turning to Elsie, he asked, 'Ma'am, what is your name?'

'Elsie,' she called out with a beaming smile.

The crowd erupted as she paraded across the stage, pushing the knee walker.

'What happened to your leg, Elsie?' the announcer asked.

'Out shooting rabbits on the farm and shot myself in the foot,' she declared.

Laughter exploded. More applause followed. By the time Elsie wheeled off the stage, she was a sensation.

Bella caught up, still laughing. 'Heavens above, Elsie, trust you to end up in Fashions on the Field!'

Elsie grinned. 'Look how many people we made happy!'

Later, as Bella placed their bets, a well dressed man smirked at Elsie. 'Who was drunk last night and fell over?' he teased.

Elsie eyed his bald head and shot back, 'My leg will heal, but nothing's bringing your hair back.'

The man scowled and strode off.

Bella sighed. 'Poor bloke. Elsie, don't you ever think before you open your mouth?'

'That's a no fun habit I don't want to learn,' Elsie replied.

They made their way to the horse stalls, where Bella nearly patted a horse before a trainer barked, 'Don't touch the horse, madam.'

'Sorry! Just wishing him luck,' Bella said.

'Firstly, it's a girl. Her name is Further North.'

'Oh! We bet on her. Hope she wins!'

Nearby, Elsie admired another horse. 'I like brown horses,' she remarked.

A voice scoffed, 'Don't think you'd know much about horses.'

Elsie recognised the bald man. 'I grew up on a farm!' she defended.

'Yeah? Probably a potato farm,' he quipped.

She refused to apologise. 'What's your horse called?'

'Danger Man,' he said smugly.

'We haven't backed him.'

'Your loss. He's going to win.'

Elsie smirked. 'Phooey. You all say that.'

Back in the members' area, they joined seasoned race-goers at their table. 'Who gave you your tip?' someone asked.

'Our taxi driver,' Elsie said confidently.

The table erupted in laughter.

Grinning, Elsie turned to Bella. 'Put fifty on Danger Man. He looks like a strong contender.'

Chapter 28

'It was getting close to start time for the Melbourne Cup, let's go down and get close to the track to watch the race,' suggested Bella.

'Good idea,' Elsie agreed.

It was a crush everywhere they walked; however, patrons moved aside when they saw Elsie on the ankle walker. Finally, they made it to the fence. It was only minutes until an almighty roar erupted from the crowd, and then the pack of horses thundered past.

The vibrant colours of the silks and horses blurred into one streak of tones as they raced by. The ground trembled beneath them, and the air vibrated with the sound of pounding hooves. Neither of them could hear a word over the deafening cheers. Bella started yelling for Further North, while Elsie shouted for Danger Man. The pack was now on the far side of the track, with horses jockeying for positions. Excitement built as patrons continued shouting, spurring on their chosen horse.

As they thundered down the main straight, the roaring

crowd jumped with anticipation. 'Go, go, Further North! Come on, Danger Man!' The buzz was electric. The track announcer screamed into his microphone, his words running together in the frenzy of the moment. Neither Elsie nor Bella knew who was winning, but it didn't matter, they were screaming with pure joy.

Hats flew into the air. Punters hugged. Genuine smiles lit up faces everywhere. The horses slowed once past the winning post, and the jockeys relaxed. Danger Man had won by a head.

As Danger Man was led into the winner's circle, cameras flashed from every angle. The jockey took his saddle and walked to the judging area, while a fresh silk cover adorned the victorious horse.

'Correct weight!' was announced within minutes, prompting another roar from the crowd. The Melbourne Cup champion, Danger Man, paraded around the circle, admired by all.

'Did you hear that, Elsie? You won! You won!' Bella shrieked.

Elsie threw her arms in the air and screamed, 'I won! I won!' She grabbed Bella for a hug, nearly toppling her off her knee walker.

'Danger Man won! Let's collect our winnings!' Elsie squealed.

Bella laughed and yelled back, ' let's go!'

The roar of the crowd and the infectious excitement of happy punters didn't stop. Elsie and Bella couldn't have been happier. Moving through the crowd was almost impossible, but finally, they managed to push their way through to collect their winnings.

'This has been the best day ever. Thank you, Bella,' Elsie said, glowing with happiness.

'We are coming next year,' Bella declared.

Neither wanted to stand around for the trophy presentation. It was enough that Elsie's horse had won.

Later that evening, as Elsie and Bella sat watching the news, sipping a cabernet sauvignon with their Uber delivered Chinese meal, Elsie nearly dropped her chopsticks.

'Bella! Bella! That's me!' she shrieked, pointing at the screen.

Bella burst out laughing. 'The one and only!'

'I'm on TV!' Elsie yelled, nearly knocking over her wine glass.

The next morning, Elsie's phone lit up with calls and texts congratulating her for being featured in 'Fashions on the Field.'

A photo of her confidently striding with her ankle walker was splashed across the morning paper, captioned: 'Even a broken ankle can't stop the Melbourne Cup.'

Emma and the twins rang as soon as they saw it.

'You're famous, Nana!' Sam exclaimed.

'You looked really great!' Stacey chimed in.

The next day, everyone in the village she saw congratulated her with cheerful comments like, 'You made the front page, Elsie!'

Unaffected by her newfound fame, Elsie laughed. 'Always been a star!'

Chapter 29

Two months had passed since the Melbourne Cup, Elsie and Bella still spoke of it with fondness, the photos from that day taking pride of place stuck on their fridge doors. So, when an invitation arrived from Michael, Elsie's curiosity piqued.

'Look at this,' she said, waving the invitation at Bella. "Wear Your Best Melbourne Cup Hat.' And apparently, there'll be two speakers a racehorse owner and a groom. Bella, you'll love that.'

Bella chuckled as she scanned the page. 'Look at Mick, getting fancy with his menu, champagne and hot chips. Must think he's hosting a degustation now.'

Elsie smirked. 'I'll have you know I'm well-acquainted with that term. I read *The Age Good Food* magazine.'

...and a door prize, Bella read out loud.

'More chocolates, don't get excited Bella you never win.'

Bella gave her a knowing glance. 'I'd be more impressed

if you didn't think two sarcastic quips make you friends with the racing world.'

'Hey, I did pick the winner of the Cup,' Elsie shot back, puffing up with mock pride. 'And I'm good with horses.'

Bella's eyes rolled. 'You don't know the first thing about horses.'

Elsie dismissed the jab with a wave. 'Details.'

When the evening arrived, Bella had insisted they go all out—Melbourne Cup outfits, hats and all. Elsie eagerly agreed, thrilled to wear her ensemble without the indignity of her knee walker.

The community hall buzzed with life. Everyone was dressed up, hats of all shapes and sizes perched on heads. As they entered each person wrote their name on a ticket for the door prize.

Predictably, Beryl was there in her green twinset with a woolly hat and matching scarf. Elsie whispered to Bella, 'That jumper will outlast the apocalypse.'

The night kicked off with Michael taking the podium, looking like he was about to burst with pride. 'Ladies and gentlemen, we've got two very special guests tonight. My cousin Adam a strapper and race horse owner Steve, the team behind the latest Melbourne Cup winner!'

'Danger Man!' Elsie's shout rang out before she could think, drawing startled looks from the crowd.

Steve, the bald man Mick had introduced, grinned from ear to ear. 'Potato farmer!' he called back.

Recognition dawning, made Elsie laughed, the sound loud and uninhibited. 'Didn't you recognise me without my knee walker!'

'Same ensemble,' Steve joked, gesturing to her outfit.

The room erupted in laughter, and for a moment, Elsie felt like she and Steve were headlining the night.

'Mick, you didn't tell us you had connections like this!' she teased.

Mick shrugged, his good natured grin widening as Adam spoke. 'So it's Mick now, huh? You hated that nickname as a kid.'

'Not around here,' Mick replied with a chuckle. 'Once one person gets it wrong, they all do.'

The evening rolled on, filled with stories of racing triumphs and mishaps. Eventually, Mick announced the drawing of the door prize. 'Steve, you do the honours.'

Michael produced a sparkly hat from the dollar shop overflowing with raffle tickets. Steve pulled a name from the hat and read it with a dramatic pause. 'Elsie!'

Elsie walked to the front,

'Ah! Ha! So your name is Elsie,' Steve said as he passed the prize to her. She eyed the package suspiciously it was wrapped in crinkled Christmas paper, with loose string. It already felt like trouble. At the crowd's urging, she tore it open to reveal a garish orange, green, and red scarf paired with a matching beanie.

Mick beckoned Beryl to the stage. 'Let's give some applause to the crafty lady who made the prize. Thank you Beryl.

Beryl beamed, bustling up to replace Elsie's elegant hat with the beanie and draping the scarf around her neck. 'I'm so glad it went to a good home,' she beamed, patting the scarf like a proud parent.

Elsie forced a smile and muttered a thank you, feeling a strange mix of guilt and amusement. She'd spent so long poking fun at Beryl, but now it was clear the woman genuinely loved her craft. Even if she wasn't exactly gifted at knitting, the joy it brought her was undeniable. Elsie silently resolved to be kinder from now on.

After the event wound down, Steve wandered over with a grin. 'Small world, eh, Elsie?'

'Tiny,' she replied, gesturing toward Bella. 'This is Bella, she loves horses.'

'Who doesn't?' Steve said with a smile.

'We won lots of money on your horse!' Elsie crowed, not bothering to hide her excitement.

Steve laughed. 'Glad I could help your finances.'

Their conversation flowed effortlessly, Steve's sharp humour matching Elsie's wit.

'Do you ladies go to the races often' Steve asked. 'No, just the Melbourne Cup.'

'What only once a year.'

'How often do you go to the races Steve ' Bella asked

'Most weeks, sometimes twice.' he replied. There is always one of our horses running somewhere. Even interstate.

Steve felt everything anew as he explained his routine to Elsie and Bella, 'you two are missing out on fun. Would you both like to join us at Bendigo for the next mid week race there.'

Bella couldn't hold back, 'YES' she said loudly.

'Bella even loves photos of horses.' Elsie smiled.

'A true horse lover,' said Steve.

'I'll pick you up at seven-thirty on Wednesday,' he said.

'In the morning?' Elsie's eyes widened in mock horror. 'That's basically midnight!'

'Better set your alarm,' Steve replied, amused.

Right on time Steve and Adam arrived out the front of the village to pick up Elsie and Bella. The early morning light painted the horizon in soft shades of pink and mauve as Elsie gazed out at the passing countryside. She couldn't help but marvel at the beauty of the landscape as they travelled along the highway, the shimmer of dawn touching the tops of the trees, making them glow with life. It had been a long time since she'd enjoyed a drive like this.

'I gave up my car when we moved, and now I'm enjoying this drive so much I wish I had kept it,' Elsie mused nostalgically. 'I had forgotten how lovely it is to drive in the country.'

Steve, sitting in the driver's seat, smiled as he glanced around at her. 'Best part of the day.'

In the back seat, Bella chimed in, Who's going to ride Danger Man today?'

'We didn't bring Danger Man along; he's way too good for a country meeting,' Steve explained. 'We've got a three-year-old filly, Velvet Glow, making her debut. This is her first trial, so we'll see how she goes.'

The boys will have her in the transporter and be on their way by now.

They fell into conversation about the horses, the talk as easy and familiar as a shared passion. Adam, from the passenger seat, explained the origin of Velvet Glow's name —combining the names of her dam, Velvet Queen, and her sire, Summer Glow. The kilometres drifted by the conversation punctuated by laughter and shared stories. As the sun rose higher, the freeway became busier, signalling that they were getting closer to Bendigo.

By the time they reached the Bendigo track, Elsie was buzzing with excitement, and Bella couldn't wait to meet Velvet Glow.

The parking area came into view, Elsie was surprised at how many horse floats and transporters were in the parking area.

'They all get up early in the racing game,' she remarked, taking in the bustling scene.

'They sure do,' Adam agreed. 'There's a lot to do before a race. It's going to be colder than it looks, just as well you brought your coats.' he added, as Steve pulled into their spot and began to unload the horse float.

Bella felt a surge of excitement as she saw velvet glow for the first time. The chestnut filly, standing at fifteen hands, had two helpers with her. Velvet Glow looked around at her new surroundings with curious eyes. Bella, standing nearby, couldn't stop staring at this beautiful horse.

'She's so pretty,' Bella said softly, admiration clear in her voice. 'Like a beautiful auburn-haired model.'

'I like her too,' Elsie admitted, 'but I'm not much for patting horses. I'll just tell her to win.'

Adam asked Bella if she would like to meet Velvet Glow.

The beaming face of Bella said it all. She walked with Adam towards the horse, and unexpectedly Velvet Glow nudged Bella in the shoulder.

She reached out to rub the horse's cheek, and to everyone's surprise, Velvet Glow nuzzled into her arm, seemingly winning Bella's heart forever.

Elsie and Steve wandered off to explore the competitors. Steve shared stories of the different horses they passed, and Elsie, feeling out of her element, listened quietly. Steve noticed the change in her demeanour and teased, 'What's got into you, Elsie? You're usually spouting sassy comments a minute.'

Elsie laughed. 'I don't know jack shit about horses,' she confessed.

He grinned. 'There she is, the real Elsie. '

As they returned to the horse stalls, they found Adam and Bella had taken Velvet Glow for a walk around the outside track. Steve unfolded a couple of chairs from the float and they sat and chatted. Elsie asked.'Have you always worked with horses Steve?'

'Runs in the family,' Steve explained. 'I love them, but I was too tall to be a jockey, so I manage the family stud. We've had a lot of winners over the years, but Danger Man was our first Melbourne Cup winner. That was Dad's and Bills proudest moment in racing.'

'And Velvet Glow?' Elsie asked.

'She's promising. Smart and eager to please. If she grows and fills out, we could have another Cup winner on our hands, but you never get ahead of yourself in this game.'

Soon, Liam Bromwell, the jockey, arrived. Steve introduced him to Elsie, and they discussed the strategy for Velvet Glow's first race. Steve was protective of the young filly, making sure Liam understood the plan no whip, just a clean run to gauge her potential.

As they all gathered on the rail to watch the race, Bella's excitement was palpable. She had placed a bet on Velvet Glow, confident in the filly's potential, despite Steve's advice to go for a place bet instead of a win. Elsie, amused by Bella's enthusiasm, couldn't resist teasing her, 'hope you are luckier than with lotto.'

The announcer's voice filled the air as the gates opened and the horses surged forward. Velvet Glow started slow, but as the race progressed, she found her stride, pushing through the pack and gaining on the leaders' Bella shouted, excitement bubbling in her voice. 'Look at her pace!' Bella couldn't contain her excitement.

Elsie and Bella were jumping up and down yelling 'Go Velvet Glow, Go.' By the time they crossed the finish line, Velvet Glow had secured fourth place in her very first race.

Elsie and Bella hugged each other, celebrating the promising debut.

As Velvet Glow was safely loaded into the transporter, the day began winding down. The soft hum of the car's engine filled the air as they started the journey back home. Bella stared out the window, her eyes tracing the passing trees and wide paddocks, lost in thoughts of the horses and the peaceful beauty of the countryside. The day had been a triumph, and she still couldn't get over how stunning Velvet Glow looked in her race debut.

Elsie sat back, feeling content.' I had a fun day', she said, breaking the silence. 'I loved how friendly everyone was at the races. You don't see that kind of warmth much these days.'

Bella, still in her reverie, smiled. 'Thanks for bringing us along, guys,' she said, turning her gaze from the window. She launched into another round of chatter about the horses, particularly about Velvet Glow's performance.

Steve, his hands on the wheel, shared the news from Liam Bromwell. It was interesting to hear his feedback. He's a seasoned jockey, and I trust his judgment. Velvet Glow's got real potential. A few years of proper training, and who knows? Maybe we've got a future champion.

As the car and horse float finally pulled up outside the life style village where Elsie and Bella lived, Steve stepped out to open Elsie's door. His expression was a little more serious than usual.

Can I speak to you for a moment, Elsie? Steve asked, his voice gentle.

Elsie raised an eyebrow, curious. Sure, what's up?

Steve took a deep breath, then asked, Would you like to go out to dinner with me on Friday night?

Elsie blinked in surprise, her heart doing a little flip.

Why? she asked, her signature bluntness catching her off guard this time.

Steve smiled, unfazed. Because I like you. You're fun to be with.

Elsie tilted her head, trying to wrap her mind around the unexpected invitation. So, is this a kind of date?

'No,' Steve said with a grin. 'A real date.'

There was a long pause as Elsie processed his words. Then, without overthinking it, she smiled. 'Yes, Steve, that'll be nice.'

Steve's face lit up, and he gave a small nod. 'Great, I'll ring you tomorrow and confirm times.'

With that, he said goodbye and headed back into the car. Elsie and Bella retreated into Elsie's cozy lounge room, after pouring a glass of Chardonnay they relaxed. The evening light filtering through the curtains adding a golden glow to the space as they recapped the events of the day.

Bella was the first to break the comfortable silence. 'What did Steve want to talk about?'

'You will never guess Bella, he asked me out on a date.'

'You've got to be kidding me! You're going on a date? 'Her voice was laced with equal parts excitement and disbelief.

Elsie chuckled, still a bit stunned herself. 'Yeah. A real date. Can you believe it?'

'Elsie, I hope you remember what to do!' Bella teased, eyes twinkling with amusement.

Elsie threw her head back and laughed, a real, genuine laugh that bubbled up from somewhere deep inside. 'So do I.'

'Bella, you know, I really like Steve. He's a good man. And honestly, I never thought he'd ask me out. I mean, I wasn't expecting... this.'

Bella's expression softened.' Go for it, Elsie. He's a gentleman. You deserve to be happy.'

Elsie fell quiet after that, sipping her drink thoughtfully. Her mind drifted back over the years, her long and happy marriage, the loss of her husband to cancer ten years ago. She hadn't been looking for a relationship, not in any way. Jokes about dating were just that jokes. But now, with Steve's offer, things felt different. For the first time in a long while, she felt a little flutter of something... possibility.

Bella, recognising the weight of the moment, stayed quiet, knowing her friend well enough to sense when words were unnecessary. Elsie, lost in her thoughts, was already considering how life had a way of changing unexpectedly.

Chapter 30

Elsie's heart fluttered as she heard Steve's voice on the other end of the phone. 'Hi, Elsie, Steve here.'

'Hi, Steve!' she replied, a smile creeping onto her face, even though he couldn't see it. 'It sounds like you.'

'I was hoping you might like to have dinner at Carla's in the city. Have you been there?'

'No, I haven't tried that one, but it sounds nice.' Elsie said, feeling a rush of excitement.

'I haven't been there either,' he replied. 'How about we say six-thirty for dinner? I'll pick you up at five-thirty.'

'Thanks, Steve. I'm looking forward to it.'

As soon as she hung up, she dashed over to Bella's house. 'Bella, Bella! I am going to dinner at Carla's in the city with Steve!' she exclaimed, her voice a mix of thrill and panic. 'What in heavens name will I wear?'

Bella laughed, shaking her head. Not your black pointed-toed high heels! I couldn't go through another Snow White catastrophe.

Elsie rolled her eyes. How about your LBD?

But I don't have a little black dress hanging up, waiting for a dinner date, Elsie protested, her mind racing.

'Let's go through your wardrobe together,' Bella suggested, determination in her eyes.

They sifted through Elsie's clothes, Bella pulling out various pieces and holding them up for critique. After what felt like an eternity, Bella found just the right thing: a light pink summery dress paired with a navy blazer.' Now that looks nice,' she declared, grinning.

'I don't want nice, Bella,' Elsie retorted. 'I want terrific.'

'Since when has fashion mattered this much to you?' Bella teased, but she could see the spark of excitement in Elsie's eyes.

'I think we should go to the shopping centre and have a look,' Elsie suggested.

Dressing the princess for her first date in 40 years, I guess, Bella said, beaming at her friend.

Thanks, Bella, Elsie replied, feeling grateful for her support.

When the taxi arrived, they set off for the shopping centre, excitement buzzing in the air. There were two reasonable shops for fashion, and both had nice window displays.

Elsie was quieter than usual, lost in her thoughts. Bella knew she had a big job ahead: finding an outfit that would truly make Elsie smile.

In the next shop, a sales lady was unpacking new stock. As she looked up, she asked, 'Looking for anything special, ladies?'

Elsie didn't answer, leaving Bella shocked. 'Yes, a dinner dress for my friend,' Bella answered for Elsie.

'Here, these have just come in. Have a look, and there

are some nice ones on the back display,' the sales lady suggested.

Bella bent down and spotted a light pink dress. It looked more beautiful the longer she held it up. Elsie, try this one on! It's so pretty.

Still silent, Elsie walked over, took the hanger, and headed into the changing room. Bella could sense she was in an odd mood today, but she remained hopeful. Moments later, Elsie emerged. 'Bella, this is it! she said, her face lighting up.'

'Shoes?' queried the sales lady.

'Yes, low and soft, please' Elsie replied, a hint of nervousness in her voice.

Bella felt a flicker of worry for her friend. Hardly talking and now asking for comfortable shoes? The end of the world must be near.

The sales lady returned with a creme pair of shoes that had a matching clutch. Let's try it all on together, she said with a smile.

When Elsie stepped out, she looked stunning. Her blue eyes sparkled, and the blonde tips in her hair framed her face beautifully.

'Bella, I do feel beautiful in this outfit,' she admitted, a genuine smile breaking through.

'Well, at least you've found your voice,' Bella teased.

'I've told you before, I see it, I like it, and I buy it.'

'Yes,' Bella chuckled, 'after I find it for you!'

It was such a relief to hear Elsie laugh again, and it made Bella's heart swell with happiness.

By five o'clock, Elsie was ready and walked over to Bella's house for a show-off parade. 'Elsie, it's a stunner! How are the shoes?'

'Not tight at all. You were right, Bella. It's time in life to have comfortable shoes.'

'Wow, Elsie! Not only have you found your voice, but you've given me a compliment as well,' Bella beamed, her excitement palpable.

'Was it worth waiting fifty years for?' Elsie joked, the joy in her laughter echoing through the room.

'Absolutely,' Bella replied, feeling a warmth in her heart for her friend.

As they stood there, Elsie couldn't help but feel a mix of nostalgia and hope. This was more than just a date; it was a new chapter in her life, and she was ready to embrace it.

Chapter 31

As Steve pulled up outside Elsie's unit, a rush of excitement mixed with nerves fluttered through her. When she stepped outside to greet him, he handed her a bouquet of long-stemmed red roses.

'Oh! Is it Valentine's Day?' she asked, genuinely surprised.

'Yes, for me it is,' he said, looking pleased. 'Elsie, you look beautiful.'

'Thank you, Steve,' she replied, feeling her cheeks warm at the compliment.

They drove into Melbourne, the city lights twinkling as they approached. When they parked in the underground car park, anticipation bubbled up inside her. The lift was nearby, and Steve pressed the button for the 20th floor.

'Can't wait to see the view from up there,' she said, glancing at him with a smile.

He gently took her hand and gave it a squeeze. 'I just want to look at you all night.'

Her heart raced at his words, and a soft blush spread

across her face. Catching a glimpse of their reflection in the lift's mirrored wall, she couldn't help but think they made a striking couple.

With a smile, Steve leaned over and kissed her on the cheek. The warmth of the moment wrapped around her like a cozy blanket.

As the night progressed, they settled into easy conversation. Steve began reminiscing about their first meeting. 'Hell, you gave me a shock with your quick wit.'

'About your baldness?' Elsie laughed, recalling how she'd teased him.

'Yep, it's not often I get surprised, but that day I did. Have you always been so outspoken?'

'No, I didn't start talking until I was ten, so I've been making up for it ever since,' she joked, her eyes twinkling with amusement.

Steve chuckled. 'You make me smile even before you speak. I never know whether to be stunned or amused by what comes out of your mouth.'

'My grandkids always tell me I should have been on the stage,' she said with a grin.

'A comedienne at the very least,' he teased, making her laugh.

Elsie shook her head. 'No, something has to prompt me into a reply, and I don't even have to think about it.'

'Don't change, Elsie. You're one in a million,' Steve said earnestly, his gaze steady on hers.

In that moment, a warmth washed over her. There was something magical in the air, and for the first time in years, she felt truly alive. Steve's words lingered in her mind, and she realised how much she had missed this feeling— connection, laughter, and the thrill of new beginnings.

Steve had thought of everything—flowers, booking

the table, even confirming the pickup time. He'd spent more time than he cared to admit rehearsing how to ask Elsie out, not sure what verbal answer he might have to swerve.

Now, sitting across from her in the warm glow of the restaurant, he was glad he'd taken the risk. From the moment she slid into the passenger seat of his car, their conversation had flowed easily, as if they'd known each other for years instead of weeks. Through entrée, mains, and now dessert, Steve found himself hanging on her every word, and feeling more and more attracted to Elsie as the night wore on. He had not enjoyed himself this much in years. He was sure he had never met anyone who expressed such honesty.

'Steve, I have something I want to say to you,' Elsie blurted, her voice cutting through the murmur of nearby diners.

'Yep, what's that, like another wine?' Steve casually took another mouthful of the 2016 Cabernet Sauvignon. He set his glass down, one eyebrow quirked in mild curiosity. 'Yep, what's that? Like another wine?'

'No,' she said, shaking her head. 'Not more wine.'

He took another mouthful of the 2016 Cabernet Sauvignon, letting her words wash over him, when she suddenly leaned forward, her expression unusually serious.

'I think I've just fallen in love with you. Honestly, I haven't felt this tingly since I was sixteen.'

The words landed like a firecracker on a quiet night, their impact sending Steve reeling. Mid-sip, the Cabernet Sauvignon shot out of his mouth with the force of fire hose, spraying the table.

Elsie gasped, her eyes wide with surprise, and then, as Steve burst into uncontrollable laughter, she followed suit.

A passing waiter stopped mid-stride, concern etched across his face. 'Is everything all right here?'

Steve, now wiping tears of mirth with his napkin, waved a hand in reassurance. He gasped between breaths, though his efforts to regain composure only made it worse.

'Elsie,' he managed, barely, through the laughter, 'this is our first date.'

'What took you so long Steve?'

His head shook from side to side, as laughter punctuated every word.

'It's not the stage you need to be on—it's the bloody Melbourne Cricket Ground, entertaining a hundred thousand people!'

Elsie grinned, her laughter as loud and unrestrained as a flock of cockatoos at dawn. 'I don't think I'd feel this tingly about that many men!'

Her quip sent Steve over the edge again, his laughter roaring through the restaurant and catching the attention of the other diners. By now, he was dabbing his wine-streaked napkin against his face, unable to stop the tears streaming down his cheeks.

'Elsie... Elsie...' he tried again, only for another chuckle to bubble up. 'I don't even know your last name!'

She tilted her head, her eyes sparkling. 'Don't bother about that. I change it all the time.'

Another wave of laughter swept over them, so infectious that even the waiter couldn't help but chuckle as he returned with two glasses and two bottles of sparkling mineral water.

Elsie and Steve exchanged a look, their giggles ongoing, the whole restaurant buzzing with their joy. For Steve, it was the kind of moment he hadn't ever experienced, the kind you couldn't plan for, no matter how much you tried.

Chapter 32

Elsie tapped lightly on Bella's door, excitement thrumming through her veins. 'Bella, are you still up?'

'Of course, I am! I want to hear every juicy morsel!' Bella's voice rang out, brimming with anticipation.

Grinning, Elsie pushed the door open and flopped down on the couch. 'He was such a gentleman,' she began, the words tumbling out in a rush. 'It was a lovely dinner. The restaurant was on the twentieth floor! You should have seen the view. We get on so well—we laugh all the time.'

Bella leaned forward, her eyes alight with curiosity. 'Are you seeing him again?'

'Yes,' Elsie said quickly, her heart skipping a beat. She hesitated for half a second before blurting out, 'I'm going to marry him.'

Bella's eyebrows shot up. 'Oh, Elsie, is this another one of your long-winded stories?' Her tone wavered between disbelief and intrigue.

'It's not!' Elsie protested, sitting up straighter. 'I looked at Steve tonight and told him, 'I think I've just fallen in love with you.' Honestly, Bella, I haven't felt this tingly since I was sixteen.'

'You said what?' Bella's voice climbed an octave.

Elsie leaned back, laughing at the memory. 'We both laughed so much that everyone in the restaurant joined in.'

Bella shook her head, clearly floored. 'I'm honestly dumfounded.'

Elsie grinned. 'Well, the quicker you let them know, the fewer girls they chase.'

Bella clapped a hand over her mouth, laughter bubbling out. 'Elsie, for once in my life, I'm genuinely astonished. What did he say?'

Elsie's smile widened. 'Well, after he sprayed red wine all over the table, he said, 'I don't even know your last name!'' She could barely contain her laughter as she added, 'And I told him it didn't matter. We just kept laughing— Steve was hysterical!'

Bella doubled over, her laughter loud and unabashed.

'The waiter even brought us water, and he was laughing too even though he didn't know why!' Elsie giggled, the memory making her chest feel warm. 'We were both hysterical, Bella.'

Bella wiped tears of laughter from her eyes. 'What happened next?'

'After dinner, we rode the lift down, and he gave me a huge cuddle and a fabulous kiss.' Elsie felt her cheeks flush as she recounted the moment. 'Then, when we got to his car, he held my hand, knelt on one knee, and said, 'Elsie No Name, will you marry me?'

Bella's eyes widened. 'And what did you say?'

'I said yes!' Elsie threw her hands in the air. 'I told him it took him long enough to ask.' She shook her head, still laughing. 'And then we laughed even more as he tried to stand up.'

Bella collapsed back into her chair, laughter shaking her entire frame. 'Elsie! That's… I can't even…'

Elsie could still hear Steve's amused voice from earlier. "Elsie,' he said, shaking his head like I was a puzzle he couldn't quite solve. 'This is our first date."

Bella's laughter settled into a warm smile. 'Oh, he's a winner, Elsie.'

Elsie tilted her head. 'What makes you say that?'

Bella's grin widened. 'He's the only person I've ever met who's your match when it comes to quick wit.'

Elsie leaned back, letting Bella's words sink in. A mix of joy and disbelief washed over her. It all felt surreal, like a dream she wasn't ready to wake up from. But deep down, she knew this was different. Steve was different. And for the first time in a long while, everything felt exactly right.

Chapter 33

Steve called every night when he had finished his chores. Elsie and he talked for hours. They shared their life stories and laughed loudly at each other's humour. Elsie was happily attending mid week races with Steve, and other social events that came up around his racing world. She was invited to several ladies luncheons, raising money for the Royal Children's Hospital.

Elsie had found the crowd happy and friendly, as she got better acquainted with the racing friends of Steve. As she chatted to these new friends she was being herself, she didn't have the desire to organise others. The couples she met had lots of outside interest that were more often fund raisers to help charities. Elsie found she loved selling tickets and raising money. She had found a new purpose in life.

Even though she wasn't a horse lover she was a Steve lover, and it worked. Steve was the happiest he had ever been, and everyone at the stud could see the romance building. Elsie was beginning to love the stud and staying weekends with Steve. She settled into his family and they all loved her extravert personality.

The road up the mountain was getting to be a familiar trip for Elsie. She loved the green gardens of the old houses as she drove past. Elsie loved the smell of the bush as they drove to the stud.

The property was high up the mountain with sweeping views of the area. As they pulled up on the gravel car park behind the main house Elsie was beginning to feel attached to the area. The main house where Steve and Fred lived was huge. A federation double story house with expansive veranda and ornate detailing on the bricks. It was picture perfect. The manicured gardens and pool, at the front of the house was stunning. Elsie loved sitting in the garden where a stand of white gum trees at the far end of the lawn, completing the picture.

———

ELSIE AND STEVE kept their proposal to themselves, and saw each other as much as possible. Now it was time for Elsie to break the news to her family.

Emma and the twins arrived for their usual Sunday visit, Sam and Stacey racing each other to the door. Kids just being kids. they pushed and shoved, determined to see who could get there first.

'Hello, Nana!' they yelled in unison as they tumbled inside.

Elsie stood with her hands on her hips, a mock-stern expression on her face. 'Can't you two walk like normal people?'

'No way! We have to beat each other!' Sam declared, his grin wide and unrepentant.

A whirlwind of energy and laughter swept over Elsie as the twins flung themselves at her, wrapping her in a tight hug.

'We'll be taller than you soon, Nana!' Stacey boasted triumphantly.

'Won't take long,' Elsie grinning back. 'But will you be as lucky?'

'Lucky?' Sam pulled back, his face scrunched in confusion.

'What does that mean?' Stacey chimed in, equally puzzled.

'Come on, Nana! Tell us what that means!' they demanded in perfect synchronicity.

Elsie leaned in, her teasing smile widening. 'Oh, just that I'm the luckiest woman in the world.'

'Did you win the lottery?' Sam asked, his eyes wide with curiosity.

'Better than that,' Elsie replied just as Emma walked through the door.

The twins, now bouncing with excitement, were relentless. 'What is it? Tell us!'

'I've got a boyfriend,' Elsie announced with a flourish.

Sam groaned dramatically. 'Oh no.'

'Yuck!' Stacey added, pulling a disgusted face.

Emma was coming through the door, she froze mid step. 'Mum, what are you saying?' she asked, a mix of shock and amusement flashing across her face.

'I have a boyfriend, Emma,' Elsie repeated, her tone matter-of-fact.

'Oh, you do not!'

Before Elsie could respond, Bella slipped in behind Emma. 'She does. Even old people can catch a break.'

Sam and Stacey stopped bouncing, suddenly serious.

Bella was the kind of person who was always right, so if she said it, it had to be true.

'Yes, she's met the man of her dreams,' Bella added, her voice dripping with playful exaggeration.

Emma turned to her mother, eyes narrowing as if searching for a hint of mischief. 'Mum, is it true?'

'It's not that bloke who tapped on your window, is it?' Sam interjected, sending the room into a fit of laughter.

When the chuckles died down, Elsie shook her head. 'No, no, someone I met at the Melbourne Cup.'

'Is he really old, Grandma?' Stacey asked, her tone suspicious.

'I hope he isn't too wrinkly,' Sam added, barely suppressing a giggle.

'Spill it, Mum!' Emma demanded, her curiosity getting the better of her.

So Elsie told them the story. As she spoke, the twins sprawled out on the floor, hanging onto every word. She could practically see their little minds spinning, already imagining how they'd retell this thrilling tale to their friends.

'And yes, Emma, it's true,' Elsie concluded, her smile deepening. 'What's more exciting we're going to get married.'

The twins' eyes widened as they yelled in unison, 'Can we come?'

'Wouldn't have it without you,' Elsie assured them.

As the excitement simmered down, the room shifted to practicalities, the twins firing off questions as fast as their thoughts came.

'What will we wear, Mum?' Stacey asked, her brow furrowed in concentration.

'Can we drink beer?' Sam added, a mischievous glint in his eye.

Laughter erupted again, filling the room with warmth, and chaos, the kind Elsie loved.

Chapter 34

The following Sunday, Elsie had arranged for Steve to meet Emma and the twins. She was buzzing with excitement, hopeful they would all hit it off. As they arrived, Elsie couldn't help but smile at the effort Emma and the kids had put into their appearances. Even Emma was sporting a lovely new dress that made her look radiant.

'Well, don't you all look great!' Elsie exclaimed as they walked in, the twins grinning from ear to ear.

'Can't wait to meet Steve!' they chimed, practically bouncing with excitement.

Just then, Elsie spotted Steve's car pulling up outside the unit. She took a deep breath, her nerves tingling with anticipation, and headed out to greet him.

'Hope you're on your best behaviour, Steve,' she teased lightly as he stepped out of the car. 'The twins have put a lot of effort into their appearance this morning.'

'Lead the way, Elsie,' Steve said with a grin. 'Let's not disappoint them.'

Inside the unit, Steve approached Sam first, extending

his hand. 'Hi, Sam.' The boy shook it firmly, his face lighting up with pride. Steve turned to Stacey next, offering the same warm handshake. 'And you must be Stacey!'

'Yep!' she replied, her eyes wide with curiosity.

Finally, Steve greeted Emma with a small hug. 'So nice to meet you, Emma.'

'It's great to meet you, too,' Emma replied, her smile softening as she took in Steve's friendly personality.

The group settled in the living room, but the calm didn't last long. The twins began firing off questions with the enthusiasm of reporters at a press conference.

'How many horses do you have, Steve?'

'Do you have any kids?'

'Did you really meet Nana at the Melbourne Cup?'

Steve threw his head back and laughed. 'Right, first one I'm not sure, because we breed horses all the time. The second? No, I have no kids. And yes, I did meet Elsie at the Melbourne Cup.'

Emma smiled knowingly, her gaze shifting to Elsie. Steve noticed and grinned. 'I'm sure you have a question that needs answering.'

'No questions here,' Emma said, her tone warm and sincere. 'I just look at Mum and know she's happy.'

Elsie's heart swelled with warmth at her daughter's words. Her gaze met Steve's, and the quiet reassurance in his smile sent a surge of happiness through her.

The moment was interrupted as Bella swept through the door, carrying two large trays piled high with sandwiches and a sponge cake. 'Look what I brought!' she announced cheerfully, setting the food down on the coffee table.

'Bella, do you have any questions for me?' Steve teased, a playful smile spreading across his face. 'I'm getting interrogated by these two little horrors,' he added, nodding toward the twins.

'None from me, Steve,' Bella replied with a grin. 'Though I can't promise they'll let you off easy.'

'What did you expect?' Elsie quipped, chuckling. 'That my grandchildren would be quiet and shy? Not with my blood in them!'

The room erupted in laughter, the warmth of family and good humour filling the space. Elsie looked around, taking it all in the smiles, the easy banter, and the way Steve seemed to fit right in. Her heart fluttered with happiness. This felt like the beginning of something wonderful, and she couldn't help but feel that everything was falling into place.

Chapter 35

Another day at the Macedon Stud Farm unfolded, a familiar yet invigorating rhythm. The air buzzed with the sounds of daily life, strapper's brushing down gleaming coats, staff sweeping and hosing the stables, others working horses in the paddocks. Perched high on the mountain, the farm commanded a sweeping view of the rugged bushland and rolling peaks beyond. Three generations had built a legacy here, their sweat and devotion woven into every paddock, every fence post, every inch of the land.

White fencing framed the vast paddocks, neat and strong, a testament to the care poured into the place. Behind the extensive stables, the training arena stood pristine, a stage where champions were made. Closer to the sprawling brick homestead, the gardens burst with colour, a painter's dream of reds, purples, and golds swaying in the breeze. Always a welcome sight.

In the paddock nearest the house, Danger Man, the Melbourne Cup winner, stretched his legs in an easy canter, playing with his stablemate, a sleek black gelding. Freshly groomed, their coats shimmered in the sun, catching the light like polished onyx and chestnut gold. Steve lingered for a moment, letting the scene settle around him, the happiness of it all sinking deep.

The news about Elsie had spread like wildfire through the farm, sparking a buzz of speculation and good natured teasing. Between the elation of winning the Cup and the whirlwind of meeting her, Steve couldn't remember feeling this content. Leading a horse around the paddock, he checked a minor fetlock injury, the steady thud of hooves against the ground matching the rhythm of his thoughts. Always back to Elsie.

Leo's voice carried across the paddock, light with mischief.

He strode over, hands in his pockets, a grin already forming. 'Hey, Steve, I heard a rumour.'

Steve glanced up, returning the smile. 'Yeah? What's that?'

'That you've been swept off your feet by a woman.'

A laugh rumbled out of him, warm and easy. 'Yeah, I have.' Just saying it aloud sent a rush of something fierce through him.

Leo shook his head, amusement dancing in his eyes. 'Well, I never thought I'd see the day you walked down the aisle again.'

Neither had he. The thought still seemed absurd.

'This will be your third.'

'No need to remind me,' Steve shot back, chuckling.

Leo folded his arms. 'She into horses?'

'Not in the slightest. Doesn't know jack shit about them. Her words, not mine.' The grin that came with the memory of Elsie's candid honesty refused to be subdued.

'Well, the rumours are flying today,' Leo continued. 'Even down to the one-knee proposal in a car park. That true?'

Steve's smile deepened as he nodded. 'Yep. Then I could hardly stand up.'

Leo barked a laugh. 'That is gold. Classic.'

'Best of luck to you, Steve.' His tone had shifted, sincerity replacing the teasing.

'Thanks, mate.'

Leo stepped forward, hand outstretched. The shake turned into a firm clap on the back, then a full blown bear hug. Steve took it, appreciating the unspoken bond.

'You busy on the twenty eighth?' Steve asked, something thrumming in his chest.

Leo tilted his head. 'Not that I know of. Why?'

'Want to be my best man?'

Leo's eyebrows shot up. 'Wow. That's an honour. Yeah, for sure! Where's the wedding?'

Steve turned, looking toward the homestead. 'No place like home. I'm thinking the garden, under the white gums.'

Leo gave a slow nod of approval. 'Terrific spot, 'Cook will be home from France just in time to do the food.'

'Oh, and I'm almost one hundred percent sure Elsie's best friend, Bella, will be your partner. She is beautiful.'

'She into horses?'

'Love's them. Always wanted one but lived in the city. You'll like her.'

Leo smirked. 'Better arrange a haircut and get the suit dry-cleaned.'

Steve ran a hand over his bald head. 'Suit's already done. As for me, my hair is always perfect.'

Laughter rolled between them, easy and full. For the first time in a long while, the future stretched ahead of him, bright and certain. He never thought he'd walk down the aisle again. But for Elsie, he was ready to run.

Chapter 36

The next day, as Bella and Elsie were about to go shopping, Bella turned to her with a curious look. 'Where is it going to be?'

They hadn't really discussed it yet, so Elsie decided to have some fun. 'At a racetrack, I suppose,' she said, grinning. 'It's where we met. Our combined knowledge of horse training methods binds us together, like two great minds collaborating on a project.'

Bella rolled her eyes, already sensing mischief. 'OMG, Elsie, it's a wedding, and only the second time you've been a bride.'

'Well then, maybe the top of a building with a view of the skyline might be nice. Or perhaps a lonely stretch of beach with waves crashing in the background.'

'You do go on, Elsie,' Bella teased.

With an exaggerated flutter of her eyelashes, she struck a dramatic pose, one shoulder higher than the other. 'And just who is going to be your bridesmaid? I wonder.'

'Not you, Bella. You're far too pretty to be a bridesmaid. You know, it's best to ask an ugly friend so the bride looks beautiful in the photos.'

Bella smirked. 'Mmm, a backhanded compliment. I'll take it, though. I'm still pretty, aren't I?'

'For an older woman,' Elsie teased back. 'Besides, you might throw me off balance on such a grand occasion. I might forget my lines.'

'Oh, Elsie, you'll probably make up new ones on the day.'

They both burst into laughter, Bella chiming in, 'I'm getting a new dress for this wedding.'

'No, Bella, that's way too extravagant. Besides, you'll be too busy helping me choose one.'

She laughed loudly with Elsie. 'Alright, I'll let you come along. Maybe we'll see something you like.'

As they scanned the rows of beautiful outfits, Bella asked, 'Are the twins still excited about the wedding?'

'They certainly are. They're already deciding what to wear. But more importantly, they want to know if they can have beer.'

Bella paused, pulling a soft blue dress from the rack. 'I think blue is your best colour, Elsie. It always makes your eyes pop. Let's look for something blue first, and then we can find something for me to tone in with it.'

Elsie folded her arms. 'Oh no, Bella. I thought I would go for a white Christmas tree dress this time.'

'In your dreams, Elsie.'

'So, no long veil over my face?'

'Some people would think that's a good idea. You'd look a little overdone for your age.'

'Guess so.'

Bella finally found a beautiful pale aqua blue mid-length silk dress with sheer short sleeves. She held it up for Elsie. 'Try this on.'

Elsie's eyes lit up. 'I love the colour, Bella. It's beautiful.'

Bella watched as Elsie tried it on, the soft fabric flowing effortlessly over her figure. The colour complemented her perfectly, it fit as though it was made for her. Bella smiled to herself she always knew what worked.

Chapter 37

Elsie practically buzzed with joy. 'I'm so excited, Bella! Imagine me getting married again, who would have thought?' She twirled slightly, the dress Bella had chosen flowing effortlessly around her. The shoes were a perfect fit, and she couldn't resist one last look in the mirror. Bella truly had an eye for fashion.

Emma had called earlier to confirm she would meet them at the stud farm. 'Your grandchildren are overexcited,' she said, amusement in her voice.

Elsie smiled at the thought. 'They will look so grown up in their new clothes. Make sure they stand close to the front.'

'Of course. I think the twins will be as close to you as they can be.'

'Is Todd driving you all up?'

'Of course Mum, Todd is excited to see the Stud Farm.'

When Michael pulled his car right up to the door of Elsie's unit, she grinned. 'Morning, Michael. Bet you never expected to be driving this bride to her wedding.'

'Never,' he replied with a smirk. 'Word on the street was that Steve swore he'd never get married again, let alone be caught by a woman who didn't understand horses.'

'Fate's a fickle master,' Elsie mused, thinking of the unexpected twists that had led her here.

Michael chuckled. 'Where did you get that saying from?'

She paused, thinking back. 'Childhood memories, I guess. My dad used to say it when he lost a bet.'

Steve had arranged for Michael to drive Bella and Elsie up to the Mt Macedon Stud Farm for the ceremony. The anticipation made her heart race.

'I'm so nervous,' Elsie admitted, glancing at Bella. 'I'm sure we'll have to stop for a bathroom break on the way.'

Bella stared at her in disbelief. 'You? Nervous? I've never seen you nervous in all the time I've known you.'

'It's about fifty kilometres,' Michael added from the front seat. 'You'll have a room to freshen up in once we get there.'

Elsie smiled, excitement bubbling up again. 'I'm so glad we decided to have the ceremony at the Stud Farm. What a perfect way to start our life together.'

Bella's eyes sparkled with mischief. 'Mmm, well, you certainly didn't think so at first. You wanted it on the top of a high building or on the beach with crashing waves.'

Elsie laughed, shaking her head. 'What was I thinking? Sand in my shoes if it was windy. And cramming all those people onto the roof of the Crown Casino building? Ridiculous.'

Bella chuckled. 'The best decision you made was letting Steve organise it.'

As they drove up the winding road of Mt Macedon, Elsie gazed out at the magnificent gardens. Tall azaleas, camellias, and ancient ferns lined the driveways into the grand houses, while gum trees draped in vivid creeper created a stunning canopy. Old brick homes with their elegant English-style windows only added to the charm of the landscape.

A wave of gratitude washed over her. This moment felt like a dream. As they rounded a bend, the hill levelled out, and they turned sharply left. The stud farm came into view.

Sunlight shimmered off the poplar trees lining the property boundary, casting a warm glow over the pristine white fencing and vast green paddocks. The sight was breathtaking.

Elsie couldn't stop smiling. 'What a wonderful sight. All those trees and the green grass.'

'Look at all the horses,' Bella said, her eyes lighting up with excitement.

'It's heavenly, isn't it?' Elsie's voice softened as she took it all in.

Bella nodded, mirroring her joy. 'Sure is beautiful, Elsie. It is so much bigger than how you described it.'

As they approached the entrance, Elsie's heart pounded with a mixture of nerves and pure happiness. She was ready to embrace this new chapter of her life, surrounded by the people she loved and the stunning landscape that would witness their vows.

Chapter 38

The wide gravel area behind the homestead brimmed with cars, a sure sign of a full house. Guests moved in and out, filtering through the house before spilling onto the garden lawn. Under the shade of towering trees, a small table draped in a white lace cloth, adorned with fresh flowers, stood waiting.

Dressed and ready, Steve adjusted his light grey Italian suit, smoothing down his grey and aqua tie. His black shoes shone under the brilliant sun. Despite his usual ease, nerves began creeping in as he moved slowly through the crowd, exchanging greetings with groups of friends. It was a glorious day, warm sunshine, a soft breeze perfect for a wedding.

Champagne flowed freely, laughter and chatter rising above the gentle clink of glasses. Steve took a sip, scanning the lively scene. Everything seemed flawless. The sun shone, people smiled this was exactly how a wedding should feel.

The celebrant caught his eye as she arrived, looking sharp in a tailored navy suit. She moved with purpose, clutching a large folder like it held the key to making every-thing official. With a practiced efficiency, she strode to the front, stopping at the lace-covered table topped with a vase of roses. A classic touch.

Steve watched as she meticulously arranged her materials, laying out papers, testing the pen, ensuring every detail was in order. It was almost mechanical, the mark of someone who had done this a hundred times, yet her precision was oddly reassuring. Once satisfied, she straightened up and greeted the nearby family. Emma stepped forward, introducing herself and the twins, Stacey and Sam.

'Hi, I'm Leo, the best man.'

The celebrant beamed. 'Nice to meet you, Leo. Where's the lucky groom?'

Leo pointed toward the mingling crowd. 'Just making the rounds over there.'

'Has the bride arrived yet?'

'Yes, she's in the house, freshening up.'

'The music will start when Bella the bridesmaid comes through the double doors.'

'Oh, that's lovely,' the celebrant replied.

Steve finally made his way to the front, standing beside Leo and the celebrant.

'Here you go again, Steve,' Leo said, giving him a firm pat on the back. 'And what a perfect sunny day.'

Steve shot him a knowing grin. 'So, we're down to talking about the weather, huh? You must be as nervous as me.'

The crowd shifted closer, murmurs quieting as anticipation thickened in the air. All eyes turned towards the house, waiting for the music that would signal the bride's arrival. Steve's heart pounded, excitement and nerves colliding in a way that made it impossible to stand still.

Chapter 39

Bella and Elsie were ready.

'Bella, I haven't felt this tingly since I told Steve I was in love with him. It's an omen.'

'Elsie, it's excitement, not an omen. Everything has been beautifully organised, you don't need to worry. Just enjoy the moment.'

'Thank you, Bella, for helping me so much and for being just like a sister to me.'

They hugged. Elsie opened her purse, pulled out a small red velvet box, and handed it to Bella.

Bella opened the lid and gasped. Inside lay a pair of amethyst and diamond earrings, sparkling in the light. 'These are stunning, Elsie. Thank you so much.'

'I'm so glad you like them.'

With a wide smile, Bella swapped her earrings. 'Here we go, Elsie.'

She walked through the house toward the wide-open glass doors, the soft strains of classical music began to play.

Clutching her bouquet of spring flowers, she stepped into the sunlight, heading towards the front of the crowd.

Chapter 40

Leo's eyes lingered on Bella as he leaned toward Steve, his voice low. 'Wow! You weren't wrong. Bella is beautiful.'

Bella fought the urge to glance in their direction, keeping her practiced smile in place as she focused on the crowd and the celebrant. The soft strains of classical music floated through the air, setting the perfect tone.

Out of the corner of her eye, she saw Steve shoot her a questioning look. Without missing a beat, Bella subtly mouthed, *She'll be here in a minute.*

Steve fixed his eyes on the glass doors, his hands flexing at his sides. Inside, Elsie took a steadying breath. Through the glass, she could see the anticipation on Steve's face, his telltale nervous gestures betraying his excitement. Leo gave him a reassuring pat on the arm.

Finally, Elsie stepped out, her aqua silk dress shimmering in the sunlight. She walked carefully down the path, her bouquet of white roses accented by blue cornflowers. Their eyes met, and she could see him fighting back tears.

She passed her bouquet to Bella and turned to face Steve, her heart racing.

The celebrant began the ceremony, moving through the formalities before asking, 'Are you both ready?'

They nodded in unison.

'Ladies and gentlemen, we are gathered here today to join this man and this woman in holy matrimony.'

Elsie felt a warmth spread between her and Steve, their smiles mirroring each other's joy. The guests responded in kind, their expressions full of happiness.

'Do you, Steve, take Elsie to be your legally wedded wife?'

'Yes!' Steve's voice rang out, his smile widening.

'Do you, Elsie, take Steve to be your legally wedded husband?'

'Absolutely!' Elsie grinned.

Applause broke out as the celebrant smiled warmly. 'I now pronounce you man and wife. Congratulations, Mr. and Mrs. Cox.'

Elsie froze. The name hung in the air like an unwelcome guest. Her gaze snapped to the celebrant, then to Steve. 'Cox? I am Mrs. Cox? Where did that dreadful name come from, Steve? I can't go around in life as Mrs. Cox!'

A ripple of barely suppressed laughter moved through the crowd. Steve's eyes widened, his mouth opening and closing like a fish out of water.

'What did you expect? That's my name,' he said, attempting to sound reasonable.

The celebrant, now visibly uneasy, cleared her throat. 'Elsie, I'm afraid that is now your lawful name.'

'Lawful…? It's awful!' Elsie yelled. 'Why didn't you get it changed, Steve?'

Some guests exchanged amused glances. Leo fought to

keep a straight face. Bella, on the other hand, looked ready to faint.

'Are you trying to think up a better name?' Elsie elbowed Steve. 'Well? What's it going to be?'

Steve's lips twitched. He hadn't expected this. He looked at Leo for help, but his best man merely shrugged, eyes dancing with mirth.

'Good filly, needs some training,' Leo muttered under his breath. That did it, Steve broke, his now red face splitting into uncontrollable laughter.

Elsie turned to the celebrant, hands on hips. 'Can't I just change it now?'

The celebrant's eyes darted around, searching for an escape. 'Well... no, not exactly—'

'Oh, can't I just?' Elsie mimicked, her voice dripping with mock indignation.

Bella let out a quiet whimper. This was a disaster.

Elsie sighed dramatically. 'How will I spell it? C.o.c.k.s?' She turned to Steve, scandalised. 'Heavens above!'

That was it, the dam broke. A trainer in the crowd doubled over, tears rolling down his cheeks. Laughter erupted from every corner of the garden.

Elsie, emboldened by the reaction, kept going. 'You know how these things go, Steve. One minute it's C.o.x, next thing you know, it's C.o.c.k.s. Then some unknown fool will spell it C.o.c.k!'

The guests lost it. Even Steve, who had been trying to keep a shred of dignity, bent over, hands on his knees, shaking with laughter.

The celebrant, pale and flustered, cleared her throat. 'Elsie, perhaps we can discuss this later... I am not sure what the ramifications will be.'

'Oh, so now you're a crossword genius?' Elsie shot back.

'R.A.M.I.F.I.C.A.T.I.O.N.S,' she spelled out loudly. 'There sure will be some if you don't fix this!'

A roar of laughter filled the air, one of the trainers with tears running down his face, was over heard saying, 'she's hilarious, isn't she?'

''Are you trying to think up a better name?' Elsie teased, elbowing Steve. 'Well? What's it going to be?'

Her mock outrage sent another wave of laughter rolling through the guests. 'Heavens above, Steve, I've got thick skin, but I am not walking around with a name that sounds like— she paused dramatically—a penis!'

The crowd roared, some wiping tears of laughter from their eyes. Steve, who had been trying to maintain a semblance of composure, was doubled over.

The celebrant cleared her throat, attempting to regain control. 'Elsie, perhaps this is something we can address later ...'

Steve, finally lost it. He couldn't even make eye contact with the celebrant; he started to giggle again. The celebrant, her face pale, paced a few steps back and forth, visibly flustered.

Elsie raised her voice, 'No, I will not! You sound like you've read one self-help book too many. What are you, a woo-woo counsellor? It's not a name I aspire to or want, thank you. I'm not finalising this service until it's changed.'

Bella's face was a mask of worry, knowing I had the lead role and wasn't about to concede. Poor Steve couldn't believe his wedding had taken this turn. He had no idea I'd have a hang-up about his name.

Now come on, Elsie, the celebrant cooed. We will do this service, then we will work out what to do.

Steve wiped his eyes and took Elsie's hands in his own. 'Elsie, love...'

She softened immediately at the word love.

'Yes, that's more like it. Mrs. Love. I could work with that, Steve.'

The celebrant, clearly at a loss, shot Steve a desperate look. He took a step closer and whispered something in her ear. Her eyes widened, then she let out a sigh and straightened up.

'Elsie, you have taken Steve as your lawful husband, and Steve, you have taken Elsie as your lawful wife. I now pronounce you man and wife. Congratulations, Mr. and Mrs. Love.'

Elsie whooped with delight as Steve pulled her into a kiss. The guests erupted into cheers.

'I love you, Elsie Love'

Bella let out a long breath.

Elsie beamed up at Steve. 'What did you say to convince her?'

Steve smirked. 'Told her this wedding was either ending in a food fight or a murder if she didn't marry us as Mr and Mrs love.'

Elsie threw back her head and laughed. 'Oh, Steve, you are such a deep thinker and so creative. That's the best name in the world.'

And just like that, Elsie and Steve had made their wedding unforgettable. Elsie beamed, knowing this day would be remembered for more than just their vows.

It had everything—laughter, love, and just the right amount of chaos to make it perfectly, unmistakably theirs.

MEET DEE GIBSON

Dee Gibson is an Australian Author who has written in the field of Numerology, Spirituality, and Children's books.

Dee lives on the beautiful Bellarine Peninsular, in Victoria, Australia.

If you have enjoyed any of my books it would make this new author very happy, if you could spare a minute to write a short review.

Happy Reading

Dee.

www.deegibson.com.au

hello@deegibson.com.au

FB: Dee Gibson

IG DeeDeeGibson

Tik Tok DeedeeGibson

BOOKS BY DEE GIBSON

<u>Novels</u>

Falling for Mr Love
Falling for the Trainer (release date 2025)
Falling for the Cook (release date 2025)
Forged Karma (release date 2025)

FALLING FOR MR LOVE

Elsie and Bella Series Book 1

Hold onto your hats. If you want a laugh and some

spontaneous interaction jump aboard and have a read, of this Fun, Flirty, romance.

Elsie and best friend Bella roll into Flemington Racecourse, bringing a dash of eccentricity and a whole lot of flair to the Melbourne Cup festivities.

Elsie and Bella are neighbours who are changing lanes in life, downsizing, to a Life Style Village.

Elsie's larger-than-life personality creates mischief wherever she goes. She's like a tornado in a meditation room.

Elsie terrorises the inmates, with her tall stories, and unwelcome quips.

Are Elsie and Bella searching for love? Have they been in jail?

Should the other wives be worried?

Definitely.

FROM AUTHOR DEE GIBSON.

FALLING FOR THE TRAINER

Elsie and Bella Series Book 2

When city girl Bella stumbles into the rural world of

horse racing, she finds herself smitten with a ruggedly handsome trainer, Leo.

After a clumsy encounter involving a forbidden apple and a Melbourne Cup-winning stallion, Bella's accidental blunder sparks more than embarrassment.

Should Bella accept an invitation to a party at Leo's stud farm?

Amidst the humour, awkward encounters, and unexpected visits from an ex-wife, they realise that in the world of horse racing, no one can predict the winner.

Who will cross the finish line first? Bella, Leo, or the ex-wife.

FROM AUTHOR DEE GIBSON

FALLING FOR THE COOK

Elsie and Bella Series Book 3
Falling for The Cook: release due June 2025.

FORGED KARMA

Forged Karma; released date June 2025

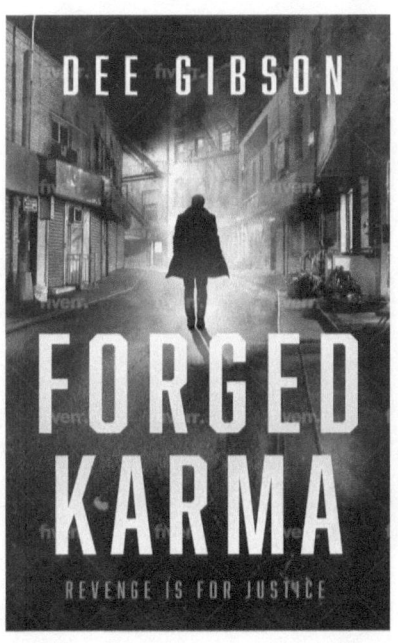

DETECTIVE CARUTHERS SOLVES CASES. He is not happy that a new recruit has been assigned to work with him on a complex murder case. This case has long tentacles, from Melbourne Australia, to the Cayman Islands.

To solve this murder, one person must give up every part of his life to bring the killer to justice.

Revenge isn't just for lovers.

Revenge is for Justice.

FROM AUTHOR DEE GIBSON

COPYRIGHT